SOME PEOPLE LET YOU DOWN

Stories by

MIKE ALBERTI

2020 Winner, Katherine Anne Porter Prize in Short Fiction

University of North Texas Press
Denton, Texas

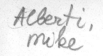

Alberti, mike

©2020 Mike Alberti

10 9 8 7 6 5 4 3 2 1

Permissions:
University of North Texas Press
1155 Union Circle #311336
Denton, Texas 76203-5017

∞The paper used in this book meets the minimum requirements of the American National Standard for Permanence of Paper for Printed Library Materials, z39.48.1984. Binding materials have been chosen for durability.

Library of Congress Cataloging-in-Publication Data

Names: Alberti, Mike, 1987- author.
Title: Some people let you down / by Mike Alberti.
Other titles: Katherine Anne Porter Prize in Short Fiction series ; no. 19.
Description: Denton, Texas : University of North Texas Press, [2020] |
   Series: Number 19 in the Katherine Anne Porter Prize in Short Fiction
   series
Identifiers: LCCN 2020029660 | ISBN 9781574418156 (paperback) | ISBN
   9781574418224 (ebook)
Subjects: LCSH: Kansas--Fiction. | LCGFT: Short stories.
Classification: LCC PS3601.L3346 A6 2020 | DDC 813/.6--dc23
LC record available at https://lccn.loc.gov/2020029660

Some People Let You Down is Number 19 in the Katherine Anne Porter Prize in Short Fiction Series

The electronic edition of this book was made possible by the support of the Vick Family Foundation.

SOME
PEOPLE
LET
YOU
DOWN

Previous Winners of the Katherine Anne Porter Prize
in Short Fiction
J. Andrew Briseño, series editor
Barbara Rodman, founding editor

For My Parents

Contents

Woods, Kansas

It's after three o'clock when Wayne finally pulls in to the high school parking lot, where Jenna has been waiting for more than half an hour, leaning against the railing of the gymnasium steps, shivering in her skirt. Wayne called her the night before and said that he'd pick her up after school, that he had something to show her, a surprise, and all day Jenna anticipated the moment when she'd walk out of school in the usual bevy of other girls and they'd all see Wayne's truck there waiting for her and she'd cross the parking lot, very slow and casual, and kiss him in front of everyone. But when they walked through the doors his truck wasn't there, and gradually the other girls loosed themselves from the group until only Jenna was left, waiting in the cold, alone.

Now, as Wayne pulls into the empty parking lot, smoking a cigarette out the window, all her excitement has turned sour, and Jenna hurries toward the truck and gets in. Without looking at him she says, "You're late. I've been waiting here forever."

"I'm sorry, baby," Wayne says. "I got caught up."

"It's freezing," Jenna says. She turns up the heater. The truck, as usual, smells faintly of gasoline.

He reaches across the cab and puts his hand on her leg. "Don't," she says. "Let's just go."

Wayne sighs and drives out of the parking lot onto Main Street. At the Eleventh Avenue stoplight she lets herself glance at him. He's wearing his worn denim jacket and his Wildcats hat. He looks tired; she knows he worked the night shift at the Valero station. She can still feel the place on her leg where his hand was, and as the warmth fades, she feels her anger fading, too. She hates being angry with him.

"Where are we going?" she asks, and in her voice is the unmistakable note of forgiveness.

Wayne turns to her and smiles. "You'll see."

Jenna feels the excitement welling up in her again. She has tried to guess what the surprise might be, but has come up with nothing. "I told Mom I was going over to Marcy's after school," she says.

"Good girl."

He turns onto Sixteenth Avenue and pulls over in front of a house that Jenna doesn't know. It's shabby, with paint peeling off the siding and a sad dirt yard. Wayne honks the horn twice and a moment later the door opens and his friend Byron comes out, and Jenna's excitement dissolves immediately into disappointment. Byron. She doesn't like him, hates the lewd, squint-eyed way he looks at her. And even worse: now whatever Wayne is going to show her will be shared with him, too.

Byron opens her door and stands there for a moment, smirking. He has a bad mouth, she thinks. He has fat lips that squirm as if they want to crawl off his face.

"Hi, Jen," he says. "Can I get in?"

Reluctantly, she moves over to make room for him.

"So, did you get it?" Byron asks cheerfully.

Wayne raises his eyebrows and gestures toward the glove compartment. Byron flips the latch and the door falls open. Inside, there is a gun.

For a moment, Jenna is stunned, speechless. She starts to say, "What," but before she can speak Byron lets out a high, admiring whistle and picks it up. It's a blocky black pistol. It looks heavy and real, malevolent.

"Hoo, she's pretty," Byron says. "She's a beaut."

"Where did you get that?" Jenna says, and it comes out like scolding. She sounds like her mother, she thinks. Her mother, who treats her like a child, like she isn't old or smart enough to make her own decisions. Always prowling around, suspicious, saying Wayne is too old for her, saying she's going down a dark road, when really Wayne is only three years older, and it'll only be two years in January when she turns seventeen. She is suddenly furious with herself.

"Aw, what's the matter, Jen?" Byron says. "You afraid of guns?"

Now her anger shifts to Byron—she hates being talked to like that—and Jenna feels the urge to get out of the truck and walk away, but she's trapped between them. It isn't that she's afraid of guns. It's that she's worried about Wayne, that he'll get in trouble for having one, violate his parole. When she met him—at the town pool that summer—he had just been released from the county jail, where he had spent three months for stealing a car—"Borrowing," he said. "The keys were in it"—and now he is on parole, which means, she believes, that he isn't allowed to have a gun.

"Fuck you," she sneers, and they both laugh, which makes her even angrier.

"She's a pistol," Byron says.

"Yep," Wayne says. "She sure is."

Then he puts the truck in gear and drives off toward the old highway.

■ ■

As they drive out of town, Wayne turns the radio on low and Byron starts to talk about his new job, plowing snow for the town—"Have to be on call day and night in case of a storm, but they pay you something even if it never snows"—while Jenna looks out the window at the bleak November fields, the long rows of corn stubble, trying to calm herself down. Their town is surrounded by cornfields, and it is thirty miles to the next town, fifty miles across the Panhandle to the Texas state line, and Jenna forces herself not to ask, again, where they are going. There's nothing out here but the old airstrip and a few tumbledown silos and maybe some abandoned barns used by the fire and brimstone Pentecostals for their revivals. Those fields: something soothing about them, she thinks, something comforting about the plainness of them, the empty flatness, the big grey nothing. She feels her anger settling into a low throb. The clocks have just been turned back and outside, already, the light has begun to thicken as it bends towards evening.

Fifteen minutes later Wayne turns onto an unmarked road, and up ahead, in the middle distance, Jenna can see a stand of trees, the only ones in sight. They pass a sign that says, "Welcome to the Town of Woods, Kansas (Unincorporated)," but as they approach, Jenna can see that it isn't a town: it's just a few buildings, three or four old houses and a barn and a grain elevator. She has seen places like this, where a few farm families came together at the intersection of their land before it was all bought up and they moved away, or disappeared, leaving their houses and barns to sag and buckle in the wind.

Wayne pulls off onto a dirt road and parks next to a large, bare maple. The buildings seem to be arranged haphazardly, as if they grew up out of the ground like weeds. The houses are in various states of disrepair—the roof of one is caved in—and there's an air of abandonment, flight. Fallen leaves are packed against the walls of the houses and windblown branches are scattered everywhere. In the ill-defined space between the buildings, she can see two old tires and a refrigerator lying on its back. The paint on the buildings has been stripped by the weather and they've all faded back to the same sad shade of brown.

"We're here," Wayne says.

"Where's here?" Jenna asks flatly.

"Here," he says, and gestures toward the buildings as if he's presenting her with a gift.

Byron takes the gun out again and they both get out of the truck. Jenna stays where she is, still unwilling to be a part of Wayne's plan. Byron walks off toward one of the houses and Wayne stands outside the truck, waiting. Jenna doesn't let herself look at him, and when Byron is out of earshot, Wayne gets back in next to her.

"What's the matter, baby?" he says.

"What are we doing?" she says. "I thought you wanted to show me something."

"Come on, Jen. Relax. I wanted to show you the pistol. I thought you'd like it. We're just going to shoot a few clips and go back."

He smiles at her, his rare wide smile, the same one he flashed at her that summer, at the pool, the first time she saw him, when she was sitting in the plastic lounge chair between Marcy and Cassie Wilson and he was standing by the concession stand, leaning against the fence and smoking a cigarette and looking right at her, right into her. She had been watching him all afternoon through her sunglasses. She recognized him, but only barely; she didn't know his name, hadn't seen him around for a while. He didn't swim, wasn't even wearing a bathing suit: he just slouched down in his lounge chair and read a magazine, and he seemed somehow apart from the screaming toddlers and young sunken-eyed mothers and the teenage boys who went the long way around the pool so they could walk by her chair and check her out. Wayne had seemed detached from all that, oblivious, and Jenna had been intrigued. Then he got up to smoke a cigarette and he looked right at her and smiled, the same smile he's smiling now—even, white teeth and the shallow crow's feet by his eyes and the dimple that appears on his left cheek—and she felt her stomach pitch and roll, and when he came over later and asked her name—just like that, no airy build-up, no cocky line—she was so breathless that she had to say it twice before he heard her.

"Come on, baby," Wayne says, smiling, and then he leans in to kiss her. Jenna resists at first, keeps her lips close together, but then she melts, again. He tastes like cigarettes and stale coffee and she can feel his stubble rough against her cheek. She loves him, the smell of him, the taste. She can feel his wanting; it fills the car. She breathes it in.

She hasn't given him what he wants yet, but she has come close, twice, in the one-room apartment that he rents over the Valero station, when the wanting became so strong that it scared her a little.

They break apart and she asks, nervously, "What about your parole?"

"That's why we're way out here. There's no one around for miles."

"All right," she says. "Let's get this over with."

They walk out and join Byron in an empty field at the edge of town, where he stands facing one of the houses, the one with the collapsing roof. A cold wind is blowing from the west, and Jenna, who's wearing just her school uniform and her light jacket, hugs herself against it.

"Locked and loaded," Byron says.

Wayne takes the gun from him and walks a few feet forward. Holding it in both hands, he sights along the barrel toward the house.

The shot is louder than Jenna expected, and instinctively she covers her ears. The noise echoes into the empty space of the field behind them. Wayne shoots twice more and a window shatters and he turns back and smiles proudly at them.

Byron takes a turn next, shooting out all the windows except for one. When the clip is empty, Byron walks back to them and reloads it. "She's a beaut," he says, and holds the gun out to Jenna. "Well, sweetie? Want to take a turn?"

The challenge in his voice makes Jenna's anger flash up again. She has shot a gun before, twice, both times with her father, though that was years ago, when she was ten, before he left. Still, it wasn't hard, and she wants to show them that she knows how. She grabs the gun from Byron and steps forward. The dense weight of it is familiar. She remembers to check the safety and she remembers how to stand—knees slightly bent, feet shoulder-width apart—and she remembers her father telling her to take a deep breath in and then squeeze the trigger gently as she let it out. She looks down the barrel of the gun, aiming at the last unbroken window. She feels them watching her, assessing, judging. The wind picks up and cuts through her jacket. She's shivering. She tries to steady her hands, takes a breath and pulls the trigger.

The recoil surprises her: the gun jerks back so hard that she nearly drops it. She blinks, focuses back on the window. It remains, unbroken. She missed. Her ears are ringing but as they clear she can hear the voices behind her, laughing.

Blood rushes to her face. She clamps her jaw. She doesn't turn to face them.

She feels a hand on her shoulder. She looks up and Wayne is there, smiling. He says, "You missed by a mile," but his voice is gentle. "You didn't even hit the house. Here, let me show you."

Jenna takes a breath and swallows. Wayne stands behind her and wraps his arms around to take her hands, the same way her father showed her. He lifts them up to raise the gun again. His cheek presses against her cheek. "Now, lean forward a little," he's saying. "Good girl, like that." He leans in, presses his hips into her. He removes one of his hands and reaches down to touch her thigh—"Legs spread a little wider, a little wider, there"—and she can feel his wanting again, smell it like fumes he lets off.

Both times, in his apartment, Wayne was angry afterwards. "Why not?" he said. "What are you afraid of? Don't you trust me?" And she said that she did trust him, that she wanted it, too, but that she just wasn't ready.

From behind them, she hears Byron laugh. "Hey, this isn't fair!" he yells through the wind. "Wayne, why you gotta be so selfish! I'm all alone here! Can't you share a little with your old friend, Byron?"

Wayne lets out a snicker, and when Jenna hears that, it's as if a switch has been flipped and suddenly she sees herself from the outside. She sees herself standing there, in the middle of nowhere, pointing a gun at an abandoned house, with Wayne's arms around her, his hand on her thigh, his hips up against her, "A little wider," "Good girl, like that," and everything else, everything that he's said to her in his apartment, when they were alone together, that he loves her, that they'll move to Wichita when she graduates next year, and she understands that for him it's all a joke, a game, a story to tell later to his friends, something to laugh and snicker about. He's right: she doesn't trust him. He doesn't love her. He wants what he wants and when he gets it he will stop caring and leave her stranded, alone.

It's as if something inside of her has burst and a warm liquid is leaking out and spreading through her gut, and she tears herself away and says, "Fuck this," sniffling, trying to keep the tears back. She holds out the gun for Wayne to take, and he takes it, and then she waits for him to say something. She needs him to say something, to make things right, but his mouth is set, frowning. After a moment, he drops his eyes from her and looks at the ground.

"Fuck both of you assholes," she says, but she stutters as she says it, and when she hears the stutter, the tears break free.

Jenna turns to hide her face and walks away. She wants to be alone, to catch her breath. Her anger courses through her like a current. She hates them both, hates Wayne's little snicker and Byron's awful mouth. She hates herself for crying in front of them, and for storming off now, like a child. But she needs a minute, needs to find a place to sit down and get herself under control.

She heads towards one of the other houses, off to her right. It's in better shape than the one they were shooting at, though its windows are broken and it tilts as if the wind is slowly blowing it over. Jenna walks to what seems to be the front door, tries the handle and finds it unlocked. She hesitates for a moment; though she knows that no one lives there, it still feels strange to go inside. Then, from behind her, she hears gunshots, and another surge of anger rushes through her. They've started shooting again. They don't care about her at all.

She steps through the door and is hit immediately with the smell, which is strong but not completely unpleasant, a mix of wood smoke and ammonia and dust. The room she has stepped into is dim; a weak, yellow light filters through the gaps in the cardboard that covers the windows. She blinks, trying to get her bearings. Forms begin to emerge. She sees a row of countertops against the far wall, and a sink, and an old, iron woodstove. She's in the kitchen, she realizes, but there is something else in the corner, too, which now, stepping closer, she sees is a bed. She walks toward it, thinking she might sit down for a moment to catch her breath.

From the field a new burst of gunshots rings out, and then there is a wild, lurching movement in front of her, on the bed.

"Jesus!" Jenna yells, taking a step back and bringing her arm up to cover her face. When she looks up, she sees a woman sitting upright on the mattress, looking back at her, blinking.

"Roy?" the woman says.

Jenna's heart is thrashing in her chest.

"Roy, is that you?" the woman says.

Jenna lets out a long breath. "No," she says. "Not Roy."

The woman snorts, disappointed. "Oh," she says. "Who?"

Her confusion makes her seem more harmless, and Jenna feels her fear recede. "Jenna," she says.

"I thought you were Roy," the woman says. "He's supposed to come back soon."

Jenna takes a step forward to see her better. The woman is wearing a thin, white nightgown. Her hair is a bright, almost unnatural red and it sticks out from her head in wild clumps. Her face is very thin and her cheeks seem to be caved in. It's difficult to judge her age. She could be twenty-five or forty.

"What are you doing here?" Jenna asks.

The woman looks back at her and frowns. "Waiting for Roy."

Jenna swallows and takes another step forward. She feels a fascination with the woman, an odd attraction. She's still afraid, but she has a vague desire to do something for her, help her somehow, brush her red hair, pull a blanket around her shoulders. It's like a finding a child, a little girl, lost and alone.

"Do you need something?" Jenna says. "Do you need any help?"

The woman shakes her head. Then she smiles. "Come here," she says. "Come sit by me."

Jenna hesitates, but the woman's smile softens her face reassuringly. She approaches and sits down on the bed. The woman is still smiling. Jenna can smell her now, her unwashed body, strong and slightly sweet.

"So pretty," the woman says. "Jenna. Your hair's so pretty."

She reaches out to touch her hair and Jenna cringes, then recovers. The woman strokes her gently. Jenna lets her. Then she looks at the woman's outstretched arm and sees that the inside of her elbow is bruised black and dotted with angry red sores.

Jenna pulls away, says, "Oh," and looks down at the ground, the dirty linoleum. For a moment, she thinks she might be sick. When she looks back up, the woman is still smiling. Jenna notices that her eyes are somehow wrong, flat, as if they absorb the light.

"Who are you?" Jenna says. "What happened to you?"

"Jenna," the woman says. Her voice cracks as if she might cry. "I'm so glad you're here."

Jenna's mouth goes dry. She feels a tingling low in her stomach. Fear. She wants to get up and run out of the room, back into the field, back to town, to get as far away from this woman as she can. But as soon as she has this impulse, the woman reaches out again and grabs her wrist.

"Jenna," she says again. "Don't."

She isn't smiling now. On her face there is an expression that is at once familiar and alarming. It's need—hopeless, desperate, unappeasable need. Jenna feels something come loose inside of her.

She rises to her feet, but the woman doesn't release her wrist.

"Let me go!" she says, loudly, frantically. She jerks her arm away and the woman loses her grip, which causes Jenna to stumble backward. She catches herself on the counter. The woman is trying to rise, too, but she's tangled in the blanket.

Then, from the doorway, Jenna hears Wayne's voice: "Jen?"

She turns and sees his figure there, silhouetted in the doorframe.

"Wayne!" she says, and runs to him.

He says, "What—" but she's on him before he can finish. She hugs him, presses herself into his body. She feels overwhelmed with relief, with gratitude. She's so grateful for him, the solidness of him, his arms around her. Safe.

Wayne is peering over the top of her head, trying to see what is inside the room. "What—" he starts again, but she says, "Please. Please, please, let's go. Please."

"Jenna!" the woman yells behind them, and Jenna pushes Wayne out of the doorway, into the fading light of the world outside. Then she turns and slams the door.

■■

On the drive back to town, Jenna nuzzles against Wayne, who puts his arm around her. "Fucking junkie," Byron says when she tells them about the woman, her hollow face and flat eyes. Her awful, ruined arm. Jenna feels as though she has just woken from a horrible dream, that surge of relief when the world is righted. She breathes in Wayne's smell. The anger and doubt that she felt in the field feel very distant now.

After they drop Byron off, she turns and kisses him, pulls him to her. She buries her face in his chest. He laughs. He says, "Well, I guess you ain't mad anymore."

They go back to his house, and she gives him what he wants. Afterwards, he lies dozing in the dark room, and Jenna lies awake, sore, naked beneath the thin, coarse blanket. The streetlight comes in through the blinds and stripes the bed. She lifts her arm and looks at it idly. She remembers the pressure of the woman's hand; the memory is a light tingle around her wrist. How scared she was, as if she might be dragged away to some terrible nightmare land. And the relief when Wayne appeared in the doorway. The gratitude she felt. She was safe now. She looks at him lying next to her, the slow rise and fall of his chest. How could she have been so silly, before? How could she have doubted how much he loves her?

That feeling lingers for several days. Then it begins to fade.

They fight. He won't say that he loves her. She says it again and again, but he will not say it. He stops returning her phone calls. She goes by the Valero station twice, and both times she leaves crying, furious.

A month later Wayne gets sent back to jail for driving drunk, and soon afterwards Jenna learns that she's pregnant. Sitting in the bathroom, looking down at the blue checkmark on the test, she can hear the TV on in the living room, where her mother is watching one of her talk shows. She can never tell her mother, Jenna knows. If she did, she would become to her no different than the women on those talk shows, who sit together on couches and fight and cry, their makeup running down their faces—women her mother calls tramps, whores. Jenna begins to cry, quietly so her mother can't hear, dabbing at her face with toilet paper. No, she can't tell her. She has to take care of it herself. No one's going to help her. She's alone, she thinks, and that word makes a sound in her mind and echoes there, the long *o* sound opening up, widening until it comes out of her mouth: "Oh," she sobs, and puts her face in her hands.

The next day, she makes an appointment at a clinic in Wichita.

In the days that follow, before the appointment, Jenna thinks a lot about the woman from Woods, sees her face on the inside of her eyelids, the desperation written there, that frantic need. The image comes to her unbidden, like headlights into the window of her mind. Like a ghost come back to haunt her. She begins to see that need on the face of others, of Mrs. Carson, the librarian, and the pockmarked girl who works at McDonald's. She sees it on her own face, too, when she looks in the mirror in the morning, and whenever she sees it, Jenna feels a sting of shame. Alone. She left that woman alone out there. Just as she has been left by Wayne, just as her mother was left by her father. The woman was scared and she wanted Jenna's help—*needed* it—and Jenna left her there, abandoned in that abandoned town. She thinks of her waiting in her thin nightgown, for Roy, for someone to come and help her.

Two days before her appointment it snows heavily, and the next day, while her mother dozes, Jenna takes her car keys and drives back out to Woods. In the car she has a box of food—things she found in the cupboards, cans of beans and vegetables and a jar of peanut butter and a loaf of bread—and a ratty quilt and four pairs of socks and a bar of soap and, without quite understanding why, a small stuffed dog that she loved when she was a girl.

The fields are buried deep in snow. The short road into Woods isn't plowed, so Jenna parks on the side of the old highway. With the box in her arms, she plods heavily through the snow, which is undisturbed, pristine. When she reaches the house, she pauses and calls out, "Hello?" in a small voice, and then again, louder. Her words are swallowed up by the snow, the empty fields. There is no answer.

It takes her several minutes to open the door, clearing the snow away with her boots and mittened hands. Finally, she forces it open and steps into the dim kitchen.

"Hello?" she says again, though she knows already that no one's there. The smell of the kitchen is fainter, just a trace of ammonia in the air.

In the corner, Jenna can see the shape of the empty bed. She crosses the room and stands looking at it for a moment, half expecting the woman to rise up from the nest of sheets. But the bed is empty, and Jenna is overcome with a deep, pervasive loneliness. She sits down and stares blankly at the floor, the cardboard-covered windows. She's come too late. The woman is gone, evaporated into cold quiet.

Outside, the snow-deep fields fling themselves out for miles in all directions. Silent, sleeping. Empty. Soon, inside of her, there will be another emptiness. And later, when Jenna thinks of the baby she might have had, she will imagine her a girl. She will imagine her a red-haired girl, smiling and spinning in a white dress, and she will not let her out of sight.

Pestilence

We noticed them on the first day—stuck dumbly to a window, inching slowly along a porch railing—but these were brief, passing encounters, quickly swallowed by the ordinary clamor of our lives.

The next morning, we woke up, drank our coffee while we watched the news, let out our dogs, dressed ourselves and our children, washed the breakfast dishes, and walked into the coolness of an April morning to meet them creeping along the sidewalks, collecting on our windshields, and dangling unnervingly in midair, suspended by thin, silken threads.

Caterpillars. They were about an inch long, lime green with a black stripe along their backs and covered with fine white fuzz. They looked completely benign, garden-variety. What was alarming was the sheer number of them, and the unsettling suddenness of their appearance in our town.

Well, of course we had things to do; no one could afford to spend the whole day pondering this mystery. Children were shipped off to school, adults to work, and the caterpillars were discussed by each group in their own private languages. In our town we pride ourselves on our modesty and humility, so we were all reluctant to offer a theory. After all, who were *we* to speculate about this strange visitation? The workings of the world are shrouded in mystery. We were satisfied to go about our days, pondering, waiting for what would happen next.

The children were especially interested in these vermicular visitors. They squashed them gleefully, then knelt to examine the splattered guts, which were, surprisingly, not green like the outsides but a cool, calm blue, the color of a clear sky in the early morning. Mrs. McConnell, who taught third grade, turned the mystery into an educational opportunity. She sent her class out to collect specimens, which were confined to glass jars and placed along the windowsill. They were all given a twig with a new-budding leaf and a bit of grass. The children lined up and watched them inch around their new homes, but their attention soon flagged, though Mrs. McConnell reminded them that science requires patience and doesn't hurry.

Meanwhile, reports came in from the farmers who lived outside of town that the event—we weren't sure what to call it: an infestation? a plague?—was wholly isolated within the perimeter of our town. The farmers gathered in Miller's Farm 'n' Feed and turned this mystery over and over, stopping their conversation occasionally to step out the door and frown at the things, which were crawling harmlessly, obliviously, around the parking lot.

We wondered, *Why?* And, *What did they want?* We tongued these questions vainly with our thoughts, but truly they did not seem to want *anything*. As we watched them crawl around the sidewalks and the rooftops, climb aimlessly up and down the tree trunks and telephone poles, they seemed as bewildered by their sudden arrival here as we were.

That evening as we made supper, many of us tuned into the local AM radio station where Bob Dorfman hosted a nightly news program. Generally, this program was dominated by high school sports and weather, and with so little news Bob often had a difficult time filling an entire hour. He would resort to recaps of PTA meetings or long-winded updates on his personal genealogy research. Alice Davidson, our mayor, was interviewed so often and so mildly that it had become a running joke. "Hey, Alice," we might say, if we bumped into her in town. "I hear Bob's really going to grill you tonight about the new pothole on 3rd Street."

That evening, though, we waited restlessly for any new information about the caterpillars. "Well, folks, I guess we're all wondering about the same thing tonight," said Bob's familiar monotone. "Since I don't presume to be an expert on bugs myself, I took the liberty this afternoon of putting a call in to Dr. Gerald Oberhauser, who is an entomologist—an insect scientist—at Northern State University. I personally wasn't sure whether he would be interested in our little problem, but he was so excited that he's going to drive up here in the morning!"

Well. The anticipation of this visit added heft to "the bug question," as Bob aptly dubbed it, and that night, as we lay in our beds, we felt that weight heavy on our chests. They were out there, we knew, hidden by the night. The very darkness outside our windows pressed in on us and seemed to squirm.

When we woke in the morning, the memory of the caterpillars felt like a dream, and we went to our doors and windows and looked out half-expecting them to have disappeared. Instead, they had multiplied. They were everywhere. They covered our lawns and streets like a roiling green and black carpet. They coated the trees and cars and even the sides of our houses like moss. They were like a strange, writhing weather.

School was cancelled, to the delight of the children, many of whose first inclination was to run out into the swarming streets and play. Parents were understandably wary, however. After all, we didn't know anything about the bugs. Were they dangerous? Poisonous? Many of us had already spent hours scouring the internet, but there seemed to be no recorded precedent for an event like this. Anyway, they didn't *seem* harmful or malevolent. If we picked one up, it would crawl innocently around our palms. Some of the younger children had to be reminded not to ingest the worms, but otherwise the greatest danger seemed to be that their clothes would stain with the crushed, blue innards.

Some older children donned their snowsuits and carried sleds out to the big hill in McCarran Park, where they proceeded to slide down over the layer of tiny bodies. It was better than fresh powder, they shouted triumphantly to each other, laughing. Soon, worm-ball fights broke out in the streets. Children made bug angels in the yard. Inspired by our intrepid offspring, we brought our snow shovels out and tried to clear our paths and driveways. Others attempted to clear their sidewalks and rooftops with power hoses. By midmorning, we had mostly recovered from our initial shock, and our natural industriousness kicked in. Caterpillars or no caterpillars, there was work to be done, goods to be bought and sold, services to be rendered. Joe Arnold hadn't missed his weekly eleven AM appointment at the barbershop for thirty-two years, and he wasn't about to start now. He strapped on his cross-country skis and glided down Main Street to the barbershop, where Floyd Norman, the barber, had just arrived to open up.

As the day progressed, we did our best to acclimate to this strange situation, and to organize responses to the novel problems that, inevitably, arose. Mayor Davidson dispatched our town's two snowplows to clear the streets, creating high, wriggling banks of bugs along the sidewalks. Many of our frailer and more elderly residents were housebound, afraid that they might slip and fall, and so the Lutheran and Catholic Churches both organized their congregants to deliver food and pay visits. Several volunteers gathered at the Town Hall, ready to be assigned a task. A crisis developed after Pete Donahue over at the water treatment plant had to shut the facility down because the sewers were clogging. After some deliberation, volunteers were sent to clear the storm drains and cover them with plywood.

By midafternoon, another issue had presented itself: the worms were ravenous. They were eating every green and growing thing. Our lawns, our hedgerows, our just-sprouted gardens, the new buds on the trees—all gone, consumed, forcing us to recognize that this infestation might have lasting consequences. No prize eggplants at the state fair this year for Mrs. Bateman, for instance, and no fall foliage if the trees didn't recover.

But despite these unhappy realizations, our spirits remained high. We strapped on our skis and snowshoes and wrapped our boots in plastic bags and plunged through our days with affability and resolve. The mood was cheerful, even festive. It was like a holiday. We felt that we were somehow being tested, and we were determined to rise to the occasion. We were attentive to the needs of our neighbors, and everyone was ready to pitch in and do their part.

That evening, we tuned in again to the Dorfman radio hour. "Well, friends," said Bob, "I think we can all agree that this was a day for the history books." Around our hearths and kitchen tables, we smiled at one another in agreement.

Then the visiting entomologist, Dr. Oberhauser, described other events that bore a similarity to our sudden invasion and mentioned a few comparable insect species, belaboring their scientific names. But the long and short of it was that the good doctor was stumped.

"It's really too early to speculate," he said when Bob pressed him gently for an explanation. "I think it's safe to say, however, that whatever precipitated it, this infestation is a once in a millennium event, completely unique in the entomological record. We'll all just have to wait and see what happens next."

Once in a lifetime, sure—we were prepared for that—but once in a *millennium*? The word itself sounded slightly insectoid, evoking a million wriggling legs. A mixture of excitement and fear swirled inside of us. That night, our minds were beset by questions. Most pressingly, Why *us*? What about our little town had attracted them? Perhaps it was random happenstance, just an arbitrary gesture of the universe. But no. We couldn't accept that. It was easier to feel that we had been singled out, *chosen*, even though that idea rubbed up against our natural humility, and for what purpose we couldn't begin to fathom.

The television crews showed up the next day. Some of our local youths had taken videos of the swarming streets and uploaded them onto the internet. Overnight, these videos had gone "viral," attracting the attention of the broader news media. Suddenly, our town was a phenomenon, a spectacle that would be shown on the six o'clock news to dilute the usual grim fare of crime and war and politics. News anchors stopped us on the street for interviews. They wanted very much to know how we *felt*. Were we alarmed? Angry? Afraid? Did we think that the Governor should call a state of emergency? Should the President send in the National Guard? It was overwhelming. Some of us expressed opinions that we didn't even know we had.

Online, speculation swirled. There were any number of theories. Alien invasion. Biblical plague. Global warming. But how could anyone be expected to extract anything sound and bona fide from that swirling whirlpool of ideas? We had no wall to knock with our knuckles in search of a sturdy stud. All we had were airy thoughts, and gutters that needed to get cleared.

Most of us tried to block it out. We did our Saturday chores the best we could (there was no question of mowing the lawn, of course, since the lawn had been devoured, and we didn't dare hang our laundry on the line). We broiled our chickens and baked our roasts and said grace. But still, many of us could not resist the urge to turn on the news, and when we did we saw ourselves, standing on the sidewalk on Main Street, holding umbrellas and speaking authoritatively, calling the government to task, voicing angry concern for the safety of our children. Through the screen, we looked ourselves in the eye and what we saw was pride and vanity. We seemed puffed-up and imperious, and when the segment was over, we turned off the sets and finished our suppers, chastened and ashamed.

The next day was Sunday, and we trudged to church through the writhing streets. Lutheran, Presbyterian, Baptist and Catholic—all our major congregations gathered in record numbers, and together the whole town prayed for forgiveness, forbearance, and strength. Both Pastor Paul and Reverend Sam preached on Second Corinthians: "If evil come upon us, the sword, judgment, or pestilence, or famine, we will stand before this house, and before thee, and cry unto thee in our affliction, and thou wilt hear and save."

After the services, as we mingled and drank coffee together, our spirits were much revived. The familiar smell of that watery church coffee mingled with an air of camaraderie. Some who had drifted away from their churches were welcomed back with hugs and handshakes. Old, dusty enmities were forgotten. Mrs. Blanchard and Mrs. Olson, who had not spoken in nearly twenty years, chatted sheepishly about their meatball recipes.

We talked of other times and other ordeals. The drought of 1987, for instance, when the sky stayed clear and blue for so many months that it seemed to acquire a weight of its own, to press down upon us with its vast emptiness, and the entire wheat crop was lost. Or the winter of 1966, when the air was so cold that it seemed to freeze into tiny shards of ice in our throats. Some of us were old enough to remember the bad years after the mine shut down, when dozens of families left their houses empty and unsold. And of course we had our own private calamities: loved ones lost to war and disease, the endless indignities of aging, children who went off to college and never came back. No, this was not the first time that we had been tried and tested, and our fortitude had always strengthened our bonds of fellowship.

As we stepped buoyantly, optimistically into the bright spring air, we saw that a change had occurred: no mighty west wind had swept the bugs out to the sea, but a strange white film was developing on the bare tree branches and the eaves of the buildings. Inside the webs, we could see the caterpillars busily spinning, building. The gauzy material was sticky to the touch and slightly iridescent: from most angles it was white, but when it caught the light in a certain way it shimmered bright green and purple, like a pool of gasoline.

By late afternoon, the webs were so large and dense that the trees resembled sticks of cotton candy. Dr. Oberhauser took dozens of samples of the material, remarking to passersby on the speed with which the insects constructed their nests.

"It's a part of their metamorphic process," he told us giddily over the radio that evening. "They're entering the pupal stage of their holometabolic development. Soon, they'll emerge in their adult form."

In the morning it seemed that our entire town was swaddled in gossamer. Not a caterpillar was to be seen, however, and although we had to clear the webs off of our windows and cars, we agreed that this was an improvement, a less disruptive nuisance. But as we went about our Monday routines, a feeling of anxiety coursed through town, a suspenseful silence, like the pause between the in-breath and the out.

In Mrs. McConnell's class, the children were distracted, looking over their shoulders every few minutes at the jars on the windowsill, where the worms had built small, individual nests on their twigs. Around two o'clock, little Lucy Jordan thought she saw one of the tiny cocoons shudder.

"It's hatching!" she screamed, and the children crowded around.

Lucy was right: the pupas were trembling. Slightly at first, and then, suddenly, they were bursting open. As the children yelled and pointed, each pupa gave birth to a moth. They were small and grey and rather plain, resembling the common moth we were used to seeing flit around our porch lights. They stood on the remains of their silken nests and fanned their colorless wings.

The children raised their eyes from the jars to the window, where the moths were emerging from their webs en masse. And then all at once they took to the air, thousands of them, millions. Those of us who were caught outside at that moment were forced to duck and cover our faces as they swarmed around us. The sheer force of them, if applied directly to one side, would have been enough to knock us over, but because we were completely surrounded, we were buoyed up, supported, and for a moment it was almost as if we were swimming in them, or flying.

Yes, for those of us who were overcome as we walked along the sidewalk, it felt for a moment as though we were ascending.

And then we were released and they were gone, rising. Small groups of them merged together into larger strands, which soon coalesced into a single, monstrous swarm above the town. It was like a great low cloud, swollen with rain. We came outside and stood in doorways, pulled our cars over to the curb to watch. The swarm moved like a huge shoal of tiny fish. It flew east at first, and then turned north, and then west, blocking the sun out completely and plunging us into a premature blue twilight. Finally, they completed a full circle around our town before setting off again to the east.

To many of us, it felt as though this loop was their way of saying goodbye. Some even had the impulse to wave.

As the cloud disappeared into the bright, clear day, Mrs. McConnell told her students to take the jars out onto the playground and open them, and as soon as the lids were opened those captives were off, too, to join their brethren as they vanished over the horizon.

When the moths were out of sight, we looked around and shook our heads. Few words were spoken. For all the bother and inconvenience they had caused, there had been something special about the ordeal. They might have chosen another town—Finley, maybe, or Cooperstown—but for some reason, they had chosen *us*. They had been *ours*. We felt the same twinge of melancholy that a parent— even of the most wayward child—feels when that child leaves home for good.

Well. We had work to do. The webs needed to be disposed of. The street sweeping had been put on hold, as had the mail. And actually, it seemed to us that larger tasks had been neglected, too, things we couldn't blame on the bugs. Why hadn't we noticed that the Town Hall needed a new coat of paint? In fact, most of Main Street could be freshened up. The roof of the American Legion looked dangerously worn. And something needed to be done about the vacant lot on West Street, and the ugly, empty storefront on the corner of 4th and Gunderson. Somehow, the whole town seemed a little shabbier than we remembered, not so quaint as it was pitiful.

As we cooked supper that evening, we turned on the radio to fill the quiet. "Well, friends," said Bob, "it looks like our little adventure has finally come to an end. There's plenty of other news to report, though. Our Eagles are playing Cooperstown tomorrow night, and it promises to be a heck of a game. Mayor Davidson will join me in a moment to discuss a five-cent hike in hourly parking along Main Street. And later on, I'll be talking about my latest discovery in the Dorfman family history, an ancestor I traced back to the sixteenth century!"

We turned off our radios, and that click of the knob hung in the air for what seemed like a long time before leaving us alone in heavy silence.

Time passed, and things went back to normal. We went back to our lives, and soon new green buds were growing on the trees again, new shoots of grass on the lawns.

Of course, we still think back often to that great grey cloud of moths circling our town, especially when a solitary moth gets into the house or a butterfly perches outside the window. They seem a little sad when they're all by themselves like that.

Though we all know that these ordinary visitors are different from *our* moths, as time passes it becomes harder and harder to remember exactly what they looked like. Every once in a while, someone bemoans the fact that no one thought to keep one and mount it in the Post Office, perhaps. In fact, young Tommy Arnold *did* keep one for a while. When Mrs. McConnell told the students to release the moths, he spirited a jar away in his backpack, and when he got home he hid it beneath his bed. At night, when he was supposed to be sleeping, he would take the jar out and look at his prisoner, which stayed alive for several days. He would gaze at the moth for hours while it perched on its twig and gently fanned its wings, trapped. And then, inevitably, one night he found the moth stiff and still at the bottom of the jar, and the next day he threw it away.

How we wish he would have kept it. But of course he is only nine, and not yet able to see beyond the small horizon of his most immediate concerns.

Two Floods

It had stormed the night before, a heavy out-of-season storm, and the river had broken its banks and flooded up onto the post road. Now the road was littered with debris, and Calvin kicked at it as he walked. Torn pieces of plywood, sharp twisted shards of aluminum, small logs and snarled clots of weeds, all lying on a bed of fine dark silt that bled out from the woods. As he rounded a curve Calvin saw a dead crow lying among the debris, its feathers smooth and its black eyes open. He gave it a wide berth as he passed. The river had dropped again—he could hear the water on the other side of the trees—and the sky was blue and very clear. Except for the soiled road it was as if the storm had never happened.

Calvin was going to Winslow's house. Winslow was his first cousin, his mother's sister's son. It was the night of the annual church barbeque, when each year the congregations of the Baptist churches in the four nearest towns got together in the clearing behind the Big M Supermarket in Speculator. Calvin was going to ride there with Winslow.

He turned off the post road and walked toward town on the state highway, where the storm had left more signs. A telephone pole was down, angled back into the trees, hanging on its black wires. At the Mahoney place he saw that a big elm had been uprooted by the wind and fallen against their barn, made a hole in the roof and splintered some beams in one wall. As he passed the One Stop Market, he looked into the dumpster and saw that it was full of food, cartons of ice cream and plastic plates of meat, things that had spoiled overnight.

The night before, Calvin had lain awake listening to the storm. His mother was working a night shift at the inn and he'd known that he'd be alone through the night. In bed, he'd listened to the wind thrashing through the trees outside and the rain against the window glass, and after a while his mind had gone blank. He'd spent hours in between sleeping and waking, aware but not thinking, the storm sound in his ears, and he'd felt absolutely alone, as if the world outside were being washed away. It had been a strangely pleasant feeling, calm and peaceful.

He remembered that feeling now as he walked through town, which was very still and quiet. Everyone had already left for the barbeque. The only sound was the hum of the cicadas in the trees. Calvin had always felt that the town was stuck in some other time, maybe decades before, when his mother was a girl, when the sawmill was still running. But now it seemed to Calvin that somehow many years had passed and he was walking through a future vision of the town, abandoned.

■ ■

At the barbeque the year before, there had been a special tribute to Winslow. Pastor Paul had made a speech, thanking him and all of the other soldiers. Winslow had stood next to him, smiling, his hair shorn short, his arm still in a cast and the scars still visible on his scalp, and everyone had clapped and cheered. That was a month after he had returned from Iraq.

Calvin had cheered, too, but it had been strange to see Winslow standing in front of everyone, smiling and being celebrated. Winslow was two years older than Calvin, and they had been close when they were young—almost inseparable in the summer when school was out—but they had grown apart as they got older. Winslow was different from other boys their age. At some point, Calvin had become aware that the boys who were in Winslow's grade were not playing with toy boats or making elaborate plans for a tree house they would never build. They were sitting around the picnic tables at the One Stop, smoking stolen cigarettes, trying to get an out-of-towner to buy them beer, hoping no one told their parents. Borrowing their older brothers' cars and taking joy rides through the hills. Talking about the girls from school, making things up. As soon as he'd become aware of that world, Calvin had wanted to enter it. But Winslow had never seemed interested. He'd kept himself apart. And for that reason, people had begun to say that he was slow, though his grades were average and he wasn't stupid. Around the time that Calvin and Winslow had stopped spending so much time together, some of the older boys started calling him "Win*slow*." Travis Benton would come up to talk to him on the street or at school just so he could say his name. "Hey, Win*slow*. Hey, buddy."

At first it had made Calvin angry—not at the other boys, but at Winslow, as if he were being taunted by

association, and it was somehow Winslow's fault—but by
the time he was in high school, Calvin had begun to feel
sorry for him, guilty even. To avoid that mix of pity and
shame, he'd put more and more distance between them.
When Winslow graduated, Calvin thought he would probably leave town, move to Warrensburg or Glens Falls.

Everyone was surprised when he joined up instead.
It was hard to picture Winslow, who was so gentle and
soft-spoken, fighting Al Qaeda in Iraq. Winslow had never
even gone hunting in the fall. He had a soft spot for animals, and when they were boys he was always bringing
home pets—stray cats, frogs and newts he found along the
river—which drove his mother crazy. Once, Winslow had
found a baby raccoon abandoned under his porch and had
raised it himself. It was as small as a kitten, and Winslow
named it Gloria and made a bed for it in his closet and fed
it milk from a bottle several times a day. When Calvin first
went over to see it—he was eight or nine years old—he
felt embarrassed, watching Winslow cradle the tiny animal,
talk to it, like a girl with a doll. Later, when the raccoon got
bigger, Winslow built a cage for it in the yard. He would
take it out and play with it, but Calvin was always too
afraid to hold it. He could remember the fear, heavy in his
stomach. Wild raccoons would bark and hiss if they were
caught in a trap. They might bite and claw your face. But
Winslow's raccoon had seemed tame and gentle, and even
through his fear Calvin had been jealous of how much the
creature seemed to love his cousin. When Winslow's father
made him leave the cage door open all night and release it
into the woods, Winslow had cried and cried.

In his last year of high school, Calvin had watched the war on the news: soldiers running through Baghdad in desert camouflage, aerial views of explosions on dirt roads, panoramas of desolate desert. He'd tried to imagine Winslow there, in a firefight, in the dust, but couldn't.

As the year drew on, Calvin had tried to imagine himself there, too. He'd be graduating soon, and there was nothing on the other side of that. The recruiters came to school three or four times a year and talked about how the Army and the Navy would pay for college. They were broad-shouldered men with even, white teeth, and they talked about the war as though they missed it. "There's nothing in the world like being in a firefight," an Army recruiter had told Calvin's class. "You'll never be more alive than that."

But on the news, the war looked hot and hard and terrifying. Every night they reported on the casualties, showed the flag-draped caskets being loaded onto planes, used the threatening acronyms: IED, TBI, PTSD. Then a bomb went off under Winslow's truck and fractured his skull, shattered his arm. A month later he was home, and at the barbeque Pastor Paul had made his speech, and Winslow had stood smiling in his uniform with his medal around his neck, a hero, and they'd all cheered. Calvin had cheered, too. He'd been proud of Winslow, glad that he was being celebrated. But he'd also known then that he wouldn't be joining up himself, and the knowledge of his cowardice burrowed into his gut. Whenever Calvin thought about the war, it throbbed inside him like a bruise.

■ ■

That spring, Winslow had moved into Patty LaVergne's old house next to the credit union. It was two stories tall with bay windows and a porch that wrapped around three sides. When Patty LaVergne lived there the house had been white, but Winslow had painted it yellow with a red trim. The house looked fresh, renewed, and it seemed the storm had not touched it at all.

Calvin had never been inside, and he hesitated on the porch, unsure whether he should knock or just go in. He tried the knob and found it open. There was not yet any furniture in the front dining room, and the light angling in through the windows made slanted rectangles on the bare wood floor.

"Win?"

Winslow's voice came down the stairs. "Up here!"

Calvin climbed the stairs and found Winslow in the bathroom, shaving. He wasn't wearing a shirt and through the open door Calvin could see his muscled body, the thick raised scar that slanted along his arm. Winslow was tall and lean and he had a long neck that bent slightly forward, as though he was always worried about hitting his head.

"Almost ready," Winslow said. "Get a beer if you want. Take a look around the house."

Calvin went back downstairs to the kitchen and took a beer from the refrigerator. He wandered through the empty rooms. The house felt even bigger than it looked from the outside. Calvin paused at the foot of the stairs, running his hand over a finely-carved baluster. After Patty died, the house had sat empty and begun to fall apart until Winslow had come back and bought it. Winslow would have gotten a good deal on the house, he thought, since it had been sitting empty so long. Still, it must have been expensive. Because Winslow had been hurt in the explosion, the government gave him a check every month. The check was for two-hundred and fifty-eight dollars. Tammy Schraeder at the credit union cashed the checks, and so everybody in town knew the exact amount. They gave him the money because they thought he wouldn't be able to work as much, due to his injury, but Pete Ferris had gotten him a job with the gas company, delivering propane, and Calvin knew that job must pay well, too, since Winslow had been able to buy the house and a brand-new Ford F-250, bright blue.

He went back into the kitchen and looked out the window onto the long meadow that extended from the back of Winslow's house to the woods. He drank his beer and thought about Heidi King, who would be at the barbeque tonight. Calvin had worn his best shirt, though he had sweated through it on the walk to town.

The weekend before, Calvin had gone to a party at Travis Benton's house. Heidi had been there, and he'd spent the whole night watching her. There had been a bonfire in the clearing behind the house, and Calvin had stood on the other side of the fire and watched Heidi through the flames, and now he thought of how she had looked, her face split by shadow, the firelight on her skin. She was two years younger than Calvin, about to start her last year of school, but she had spent most of the night talking to Sam Mitchell. At Travis Benton's parties people were known to sneak off into the woods together, lie down in a bed of ferns. Calvin had tried to get up the nerve to talk to her—drinking beer and whiskey with Coke—but around midnight he'd stumbled off to the woods to be sick. Afterwards, he'd lain down in the tall grass at the edge of the clearing and looked up at the sky, the spinning stars, before falling asleep. Then, to his surprise, it had been Winslow shaking his arm, ready to take him home.

From behind him, now, Winslow said, "How do I look?"

Calvin turned. Winslow was wearing a bright green shirt, tropical, one of several such shirts that he owned. He'd been wearing them for so long that they'd become a kind of signature, like a uniform, and people hardly commented on them anymore. Calvin couldn't imagine himself wearing a shirt like that, but he smiled and said, "You look good, Win. Let's go."

When they walked onto the porch, Calvin realized that Winslow's driveway was empty.

"Hey, where's your truck?"

"Oh, right," Winslow said. "I forgot to tell you. I loaned it out to Travis this morning."

Calvin frowned. "Loaned it out? What for?"

"He needed it to help the Purdys," Winslow said. "I guess they got their tractor stuck in the mud after the storm. He said if he couldn't get it back in time we should just walk over to the Purdys' and pick it up on our way."

Calvin paused, thinking back to the weekend before, at Travis's party, after Winslow had arrived to take him home. Hazily, he remembered walking back through the clearing, leaning on Winslow's arm. The fire had died down,

but he could see two figures sitting on the other side—
Sam and Heidi, he thought—their faces hidden in flickering shadow. Two more figures were standing out of focus
near Winslow's truck. As he approached, they clarified
into Travis and his sister, Jean. Jean had always been the
prettiest girl in town. Right after she graduated, she'd run
off and married an out-of-towner, a screenwriter who was
renting a cabin for the summer, and a year later he'd left her
and she'd come back alone. Now, she was seeing Winslow.
Calvin realized dimly that Winslow must be bringing her
home from a date.

"Hope he doesn't get sick in your truck, Win," she said
as Winslow helped him into the cab.

"Yeah, *Win*, I hope he doesn't mess up your nice new
truck."

That was Travis's voice, sneering, unmistakable. In
the glow of the headlights, Calvin could see him leaning
against the hood. No one spoke. Calvin, drunk as he was,
could sense a tautness in the silence. He sensed some kind
of menace, foreboding.

But then Winslow looked at Calvin through the window and said, "Cal, just let me know if you need to be
sick and I'll pull over, okay?" He walked around Travis to
the driver's side and got in. Jean followed him, leaned in
through the open window, and kissed him on the cheek.
Then Winslow started the engine and backed out of the
driveway, and Calvin watched Travis's slouched figure
receding in the headlights.

Maybe, Calvin thought now, he'd misjudged the
moment. He'd been drunk, after all. Maybe there hadn't

been anything to it. When they were younger, Travis had been one of the boys who'd taunted Winslow, but that was before Winslow had gone to Iraq.

Still, Calvin felt a knot tighten in his stomach. "Why's Travis helping the Purdys?"

Winslow looked at him. "He does a little work for them sometimes," he said. "Thought you knew that. Same as I used to do."

The Purdys lived on a big spread of land along the river. Seth Purdy had been a chiropractor in New York City, and he and his wife had moved up to Carthage a few years earlier and started a small hobby farm. They were thought to be a little strange, but good natured. When Winslow got back from Iraq, they'd hired him to do odd jobs before he got his job with the gas company.

"Right," Calvin said. "I forgot that."

"You know how they bought all those alpacas last year?" Winslow said.

"Yeah."

"Well, you know how their pasture was right down next to the river? I ran into Tammy Schraeder today and she said the water came up so fast they couldn't get them out in time."

"They drowned?" Calvin said, suddenly alarmed.

Winslow nodded. "Not all of them. They can swim, I guess. Tammy thought maybe one or two. The babies."

"Shit."

Calvin was surprised at how saddened he was. He didn't know the Purdys well, but he'd always liked looking at the alpacas when he drove past their place. He liked how strange and out-of-place they seemed there, their long necks sticking up across the field.

"I about started crying when I heard that," Winslow said. There was a little hitch in his voice, and when he heard it, Calvin felt his own sadness turn to irritation. He remembered how Winslow had wept about his pet raccoon. It would be just like Winslow, Calvin thought—the Marine, the war hero—to get choked up over some rich people's dead alpacas.

"Jesus, Win." Calvin said. He heard the anger in his voice and tried to soften it, to sound like he was joking. "Don't start blubbering on me now."

Winslow shook his head and sighed. "I just liked looking at them when I drove past."

They were almost at the edge of town and hadn't seen a single person. The Purdys' farm was on the way to Speculator, about a mile outside of town. They would have to walk over the causeway which ran across Lake Abanakee.

Calvin felt ashamed that he'd gotten irritated at Winslow. After a few moments of silence, he said, "Kind of weird, town so empty like this."

Winslow nodded. "Some fucking storm."

It was still hot and there was no breeze, but the sky had turned a cooler blue and around them the light had begun to thicken.

■ ■

For a while they walked in silence. Calvin felt uncomfortable, not sure what to say or ask.

Though he saw Winslow often—ran into him in town, had dinner at his aunt's house some Sundays—Calvin realized that he hadn't been alone with him since he got back from Iraq, that they hadn't really talked all year.

"How are things with you and Jean?" he asked finally.

"Good," Winslow said. "Real good. Did you ever think, back in high school, I'd be dating Jeannie Benton?"

Calvin snorted. "No, Win. I can't say that possibility ever crossed my mind."

"What about you? Think Heidi's going to be there tonight?"

"What do you mean?" Calvin said, surprised.

Winslow laughed. "Last weekend, when I picked you up, you were talking about her in the truck on the way home. Going on and on." Calvin was embarrassed. He'd forgotten that.

"I was drunk," he said.

Winslow laughed. "Yes, you were. Grandpa would've said you were chock-a-block."

Calvin smiled. Their grandfather was an old lumberman who took a plug of whiskey in his morning coffee right up until he died at ninety.

"He would've said I had more sail than ballast," Calvin said.

"He would've said you were all mops and brooms."

Their laughter echoed off the trees. Behind them, Calvin heard the noise of an engine. He turned and saw a tractor-trailer coming down the road, and they moved to the other lane to let it pass. As it roared by, the driver pulled his horn. Since they had built the new highway from Utica to Watertown, not many trucks passed that way, but once in a while one did, an old driver who remembered the old route.

After the truck passed, Calvin said, "Anyway, it's different. With Heidi."

"What is?"

He paused, breathed in, thinking how to explain. If he had been in Winslow's position, Calvin thought, if he had come back from the war and got a house and a decent job and a check every month in the mail, he would have no trouble talking to Heidi King. But Calvin lived with his mother and the only work he had been able to find since graduating was grooming the slopes at Gore Mountain in the winter, and he'd only gotten that job because his mother, who worked at the hotel there, had asked the manager for a favor. Travis Benton worked there, too, and all winter Travis had picked Calvin up at his mother's house off the post road at ten o'clock at night and they had driven to the mountain and then spent six hours in the cold with the spotlights glaring, driving the groomers up and down the slopes. Travis often had a bottle of something with him, and they would drink from it between runs. Then they would drive back to town just as it was starting to get light, when Calvin's mother was getting ready to leave and drive the other way to the mountain. That job had ended in April, and he hadn't been able to find anything else since.

"Never mind," he said. "I think she's with Sam, anyway."

They reached the causeway and the woods broke open onto Lake Abanakee, which spread out into the distance on either side of the road, clear and calm and glimmering in the sinking sun. The causeway was a narrow road that stretched across the lake, and Calvin wondered what the other road was like, in Iraq, where Winslow's truck had been bombed.

Winslow had never said anything about it, and Calvin had never asked.

"What was it like over there?" Calvin asked. "I mean, in Iraq. What was it like?"

Winslow let out a long breath and frowned. After a moment, he said, "It's hard to describe. It's probably different from what you'd think."

Calvin swallowed. He felt strangely nervous. "Were you scared?" he asked.

"Oh, yeah," Winslow said. "All the time. You're always scared, but," he paused, "at the same time, you're always a little bored. Like, most of the time, there's nothing to do, but you always have to be ready for something to happen. And then, even when something happens, and you're so scared you think you might shit yourself, you know if you fuck up someone might get blown up or shot."

Calvin was quiet for a moment, thinking. "So, did someone fuck up?" he asked. "When you got hit?"

"No," Winslow said. "That road got swept the night before. They must have placed the bomb in the morning. Sometimes shit would just happen like that. Bad luck. No one's fault."

They reached the end of the causeway and the woods grew out to the road again, tamaracks and tall pines. It was a relief to be walking in the shade, the long shadows of the trees across the road, the throb of insects in the trees, the sky tapered to a blue ribbon overhead.

At the top of a low hill, the First Baptist Church came into sight, a plain square building, white paint bright in the sun. The light caught the single stained-glass window that faced the road, and the red glass flashed in the sun like a cardinal diving. In front of the building was an old lightning-struck elm, the core blown out and a deep black scar twisting down the hollow trunk. The Purdys' farm was just beyond the church, around the next curve.

But as they passed the church, Calvin saw a pickup truck parked in a small clearing that was used for picnics and barbecues. Winslow's truck, bright blue and shining in the light. They both stopped walking, planted rigid in their steps.

Calvin could see that there was something on the windshield. It was yellow and white. He didn't understand what it was.

Then he did. It was one of the Purdys' alpacas. They had dressed it in a bright yellow shirt and Calvin could see that its face was painted. Its mouth was outlined in red paint. Its mouth hung open. Its four legs were splayed on the windshield. Its head hung down over the hood of the truck, dangled horribly on its limp neck.

■ ■

The baby alpaca's body was bloated, its fur matted and stained. Its legs had been pulled from their joints so that it would lie flat on its belly against the glass. A rope was tied around the back legs and through the open windows of the truck.

"Jesus," Calvin said. His heart thrashed like a small bird against the cage of his ribs. His mouth was dry. He began to talk, rapidly, without thinking. "Jesus Christ, Win. Win. What? What the fuck? Jesus, Win."

Winslow was silent, looking at the alpaca.

"Win!" Calvin shouted, his voice pitched with hysteria. "Win! Winslow!"

But still Winslow said nothing, did nothing, his face like a stone. And suddenly Calvin was furious. His stomach churned with anger, and it surged up his throat and out of his mouth. "You're so stupid!" Calvin heard himself yell. "You're so fucking dumb, Winslow! Why'd you give them your truck? Don't you know that Travis hates you? Jesus, Win, he hates your fucking guts! Of course he was going to do something like this! You're just too fucking dumb to see it. You're just as dumb as a goddamn—"

Without looking at him, Winslow extended his arm and, like a spring uncoiling, hit Calvin hard in the gut. Calvin felt all of his air go out, and he sat down in the dirt.

It took a minute for his breath to come back, and while he was gasping on the ground Winslow didn't move. He stood still, staring at the dead animal. When his stomach finally loosened and the air rushed into his lungs, Calvin started crying, weeping hard and openly, gasping, unable to speak through his sobs.

Winslow moved toward the truck and began to untie the alpaca from the windshield. Still crying, Calvin managed to stand up. "Win," he said, but Winslow held up his hand. "Cal, you'd better step back a minute," he said. "Just give me a minute alone now." His voice was firm but soft, almost gentle. As if he were speaking to a child.

Calvin took a breath and wiped his eyes. He wanted to sit down somewhere, just sit and breathe for a while, get his bearings.

He turned and walked back towards the church, planning to sit down on the front steps, but then he thought to try the door. It was open.

Inside, it was cool and dim and quiet, and the red-stained light from the window played on the varnished wood of the pews and the cross that hung behind the pulpit. Calvin wiped his eyes with his sleeve and sat down in the back row of pews. His heart was still pounding. His anger coursed through him like a current. He closed his eyes and took long breaths, his stomach aching where Winslow had hit him.

He thought back to that winter, to one night on the mountain when he and Travis had sat together in the groomer, drinking whiskey. Travis had been complaining about Winslow. "Maybe I should go bang my head," he'd said. "Then I wouldn't be freezing my balls off here with you."

Calvin hadn't said anything. He'd just nodded, taken the flask when Travis offered it to him. He'd understood what Travis meant. He and Travis were the same: no job, no prospects, just wasting away, stuck in that damn town which itself was stuck in some other time. Seeing all that Winslow had now made their own situation seem even more pathetic.

In the quiet of the church, Calvin felt his anger burning off, evaporating into shame. He hadn't known what Travis was going to do to Winslow that night, but he was still guilty. His guilt stretched back before that day, before that winter, back to when they were kids, when he'd listened to Travis and the others tease Winslow and hadn't said anything. When he'd watched the gap open up between him and Winslow, and watched it grow, and felt relieved.

Calvin could see the rest of his life line up in front of him. Nothing was going to change. Travis was always going to be bad. Winslow was always going to be an easy target. And Calvin was always going to be a coward, too scared to do anything except stay in that town, where his life would continue to bleed itself out until it was empty, over.

He looked up at the cross behind the pulpit, half-shadowed in the fading light. He took a breath of the still air. It was strange to be in the church by himself, so quiet. It reminded him of how he'd felt the night before, during the storm: the sense that when he woke the world he knew would be wiped clean and he'd be born into a new world, bright and blank.

He wanted that: to start over, alone. Travis and Sam and Heidi, the Purdys and their alpacas, the abandoned gas station with the rusting pumps and the empty building where the supermarket used to be. That whole pitiful town. All of it gone, washed away.

The church seemed to hum in its silence. Suddenly, Calvin knew what he needed to do. The answer presented itself to him so forcefully that it was as if it had been spoken to him, whispered through the dense quiet. He felt a steadiness spread through him, a calm resolve.

He heard the sound of Winslow's truck starting outside, and then a moment later the horn sounded twice, and Calvin got up and walked out to the truck. Through the glowing twilight Calvin could see the alpaca curled in the truck bed as if sleeping. He got in. Winslow sat looking straight ahead.

"Win," he said, his voice steady now. "I'm sorry. I'm sorry I said those things. I didn't mean them."

Winslow turned his head slowly towards him. His eyes were sad, but not angry.

"Sorry I hit you, Cal. I had no right to do that."

"Yes," Calvin said. "Yes, you did."

"Well, I'm sorry anyways."

For a moment they sat in silence. Then Winslow put the truck in gear and headed back towards town.

■ ■

Winslow wanted to bury the alpaca in the clearing behind his house, so in the gathering dusk they took shovels from his garage and began to dig. For a while, they dug together in silence.

Calvin worked hard, sweating. He was glad for something to do, for the calming, steady rhythm of the work. The rain-soft soil came up easily, and after half an hour the hole was three feet deep and they had reached the hard clay. By then, it was full blue night, but the moon was bright and there were no clouds. Winslow stopped digging and sat down on the edge of the hole. Calvin looked at him. He was breathing hard and holding his right arm.

"You okay, Win?" Calvin asked.

"Yeah," Winslow said. "Sometimes it just flares up like this."

Somehow, after everything, Calvin was surprised. Of course, he'd known that Winslow had gotten hurt—he'd seen the cast and the scars himself—but Winslow had never seemed to be in any pain. "Okay," he said. "I'll finish up here."

"No, that's deep enough," Winslow said. He walked over to the truck and lifted the dead alpaca out of the bed and carried it gently in his arms, like a baby. He stepped down into the hole and lay the animal in the dirt. Then he climbed out and they stood there for a moment, looking at it in the moonlight. It looked small, dead. It still wore the yellow shirt. Calvin looked at Winslow. His own bright green shirt was dirty, smeared with mud. Calvin saw that Winslow was crying. Quietly, just leaking tears.

"Win," he said.

Winslow shook his head and sighed. He wiped his face with his sleeve. Then he picked up his shovel and began filling in the grave. Calvin paused, not knowing what to say. After a moment, he started shoveling, too. When the grave was filled, they put the shovels away and stood in the glow of the spotlight above the garage door.

Winslow put a hand on Calvin's shoulder and said, "See you soon."

"Win, listen," Calvin said. "I've been thinking about joining up."

"What?" Winslow said, frowning.

"Joining up."

Winslow's face relaxed and he let out a long, slow breath.

"I can't find any work," Calvin said. "This town is dead. There's nothing here for me."

"Listen, Cal," Winslow said after a moment. "It's not like you think, over there. It's not all guts and glory."

"I know."

"No, you *don't* know." There was a tinge of anger in Winslow's voice now. He turned his face away, frowning. When he looked back at Calvin, though, his expression was blank, unreadable. Calvin waited. "It's been a hard night," Winslow said. "Let's talk about it another time."

Calvin nodded and turned and walked out to the road and through town. Everyone had returned from the barbeque. Lights shone out of the windows, and Calvin heard laughter drifting out of the Oak Barrel. People were sitting on their porches, playing music. Cars and trucks beeped their horns when they passed him on the highway. Calvin felt strangely apart from all of them, as though he'd already left. In the morning, he'd go out to the recruitment center in Warrensburg. He wasn't afraid. In fact, he felt relieved, unburdened.

He walked slowly back down onto the post road, where there were no lights, and he could feel the silt beneath his feet and hear the river flowing softly behind the trees, restored to its usual gentleness.

■ ■

Midsummer a year later, Calvin's platoon was camped next to another river, in a small village in Baghlan Province, Afghanistan, one of many villages of mud-brick houses along a narrow valley. During the day they worked digging a large hole that would serve as a kind of septic tank and putting up a flimsy wooden building that would be a school. At night they camped by an irrigation canal outside the village.

During their second week in the village it began to rain. It was late at night and Calvin heard the rain in the fig trees overhead before he felt it. They heard over the radio that other villages upriver were flooding, and an hour later the canal had risen visibly. They moved their camp into the village. The river, which had been slow and idle, was loud now with surge, and after another hour it had cleared its banks. The company squatted in the mud of the village square and the villagers brought their livestock to higher ground. An elderly man came to Lieutenant Drake and asked him for help, and then they all went to work.

Some animals were already stuck in the water and the mud, goats and cows stranded, bellowing. Calvin and some others were working with shovels along the bank, trying to build a barrier out of earth. From across the black water he heard bleating, and in the moonlight he could see a goat standing on a small sandbar, crying out.

Calvin dropped his shovel and waded into the river alone. When he got to the island the water came to his chest and he picked up the kicking goat and carried it bleating back across to the bank. The goat's owner smiled at him and said something that he thought meant thank you.

They worked through the night as the river kept rising. The worry was that the water would reach the village itself, but near morning the rain stopped, and an hour later it dawned a clear, bright day, and by afternoon the river had dropped and the danger had passed. Everyone was cheerful. They stood around in the trees, drinking water, eating figs from the branches, joking. Children played among them.

Winslow had been right: the war wasn't like Calvin had imagined it. Calvin knew soldiers were getting shot at and blown up elsewhere, but his company spent most of its time building schools and digging latrines and handing out gifts to children, baseball hats and maps of Afghanistan. More than once, he'd heard other soldiers gripe about it. They wanted the war they had seen on TV. Calvin felt that way, too, sometimes. His war wasn't about honor and courage and glory. His war was just work. So for the rest of the year, through the winter and the spring, Calvin kept the night of the flood in his mind: a small, clear victory, something to tell Winslow when he got home.

In the summer of his second year the company returned to the same village and found it abandoned. The fighting had been heavy over the winter, and many people had left their homes. The building they'd built as a school had been stripped for wood. Calvin walked through the brown mud houses, found small things left there, trash, a broken shovel, a teacup and saucer on a wooden table. Calvin could sense a general feeling of discouragement among the company. The flood had been something they'd talked of often. They'd all been holding onto it, as Calvin had.

But now they saw that it had been for nothing.

Calvin's deployment would be up in six months. Then he could re-enlist or go home. Every week, his mother wrote him an email with news from home, though it was hardly news. Everything sounded the same as always. The only notable information he'd gotten was that Winslow and Jean would be getting married in September. Calvin would miss the wedding, but he didn't mind. The thought of returning home from the war and resuming his old life filled him with a tingling dread, a metallic sting in his mouth.

Since the houses were empty they slept inside instead of by the canal. That night, Calvin had a dream. He was in that same empty village, walking through the houses just as he'd done that day, searching for something. He entered a house and mounted on the wall, like a trophy, was the alpaca's head, its painted face. It turned its neck and looked at him with huge, round, black eyes. And then it began to laugh.

He startled awake and left the house. It was still dark. The night was warm, and he walked down to the river where it was cooler. Calvin sat on the bank for a long time. He closed his eyes and tried to remember what he'd felt the night of the first flood, alone in his room in his mother's house with the storm seething outside. The sense that everything was being washed away. That complete aloneness, that peace. But he couldn't conjure that feeling whole; he could only touch the edge of it. Instead, his dream-vision hovered in his mind. It stared at him with its black eyes, laughing. Calvin could still see the alpaca's painted face, still hear its awful cackle.

As the pale light bloomed across the valley, he watched the river: low and slow-moving, a brown cloud drifting down from the mountains. There had been a drought that summer. Soon, the true dry season would arrive, and it would last for a long time.

Kid Kansas

Summer was over. They all knew it. Each had noticed that subtle shift—nighttime chill still clinging midmorning to metal and glass, pale ghost of breath floating up from the mouth at dawn—which is why they'd gathered there, in a sprawling, weed-filled lot near the railyard outside of Erie, with the broad shadow of a plastics factory looming over them, on what might have been the last warm night of the season. It happens every year, this assembly, a kind of ritual, in late September or early October, in one blighted city or another—earlier that day, huddled in the empty freight car, Byron had counted back through the years in his mind: Buffalo, Gary, Sheboygan, Scranton, and so on—a tradition that stretched well beyond his remembering. Who can say what drew them, exactly, though Byron believed that all traditions must have their roots in instinct, including this one: in some prehistoric desire to come together as the dark season advanced, celebrate the harvest and bid farewell to the sun before the real winter settled in.

Personally, Byron had felt it a few days earlier—gazing up at the evening sky, he'd seen in it a new iron quality, wintry undertone—and so he'd thumbed-it down from the apple-picking regions of Vermont to Albany, where he'd lingered until he heard word of the date and location of that year's rendezvous, after which he hopped the freight and rode it through the night to be present at the railyard, where now they were laughing, drinking sweet wine, sharing tips—the bulls around Chicago get meaner every year; there's good winter work to be found in Idaho, cutting timber, if you don't mind the cold—and telling stories.

Among the familiar faces around the meager, unnecessary barrel fire—Pockmarked Lewis and Red and Mississippi Jerry and Murph and Black and White Tony, who always travelled together—there were some new ones, too, and one in particular that Byron was watching: a fresh-faced white kid, seventeen maybe, who sat at the edge of the crowd, not speaking, but—you could tell from the way he sat, pitched forward on his crate, and by the way his eyes shone—listening intently. Byron searched his face, which in the firelight's soft lambency seemed familiar, though he couldn't identify any particular antecedent. He'd seen too many young kids like him over the years, green as saplings, in flight from home—on the lam, maybe, Byron thought, after a gas station robbery yielded nothing but a few rumpled twenties and change, or maybe run off when Dad found the wrong kind of magazine under his bed, or maybe just a dirt-farm kid from South Dakota who took a hard look at his situation and decided, sensibly, to skedaddle, kiss Mom on the cheek and vanish into the purple dusk—ribs sore from sleeping on the ground for the first time, bright with hunger and fear and innocence, not yet carrying any kind of weapon, and eager, desperate, for any kind of information: the kind of stray tip, dropped as thoughtlessly as a used match, that might provide some direction in the great uncertainty, lead him south instead of west.

Oh, this kid was listening, all right, eyes shining, greasy lank of hair sagging over his brow—he'd been on the road a few weeks, Byron estimated, probably took off just after his last haircut—and so Byron tuned in, too. That fiend was known to swig turpentine if that's all there was to hand, Murph said in his well-worn rasp, and Byron knew immediately that they were talking about Angel Garcia, Little Angel. So oriented, he could see the contours of the conversation spread out before him like a map he'd memorized. He'd been around long enough that you could drop him cold into the tramp-talk and he'd know where it was headed as surely as if it had already happened, because, of course, it had.

They were now in the soft, merry phase of the night reserved for paying tribute, recounting legends, memorializing the lost soldiers of the road, and from Little Angel they'd move, probably, to Poor George, that other proud Okie, and from there to Buster Genovese, and then, following the line of ethnicity, to Vinny "Kid" Colombo, and from there they'd land, inevitably, on Kid Corrigan, AKA The Carjack Kid, Kid Kansas, and The Duke.

Suddenly, Byron felt the atmosphere change. The air itself became iridescent, shimmering, and then Byron saw a figure appear at the periphery of the circle. It was Corrigan, unmistakable, not flesh and bone but specter, a silent, lurking presence. Byron was not surprised to see him: this kind of conjuring happened to him more and more now in his advanced age, and had something to do, he feared, with the other kind of black magic that bloomed now in his body, that tumorous swirling in his lungs. Corrigan's face was slack, impassive—he wasn't staring at Byron, or at anything in particular—but Byron sensed a sadness about him, a loneliness he found both unsettling and familiar. Then the ground beneath them began to quake with a train's approach and, as though startled away, The Carjack Kid vanished into the shadows.

While the train clanked slowly into the yard, the conversation around the fire moved gleefully through Angel's other ignominious exploits, but Byron wasn't listening. He'd heard all these stories before, many times, and besides, he was thinking about Kid Kansas, because he'd come to believe that these ghostly visitations had import, purpose. Just last month he'd seen his old Uncle Albert in the orchard, a lonely, bowlegged figure standing between two rows of trees, hat cocked, squinting in the sun. Albert was the one who'd first introduced him to the road. He'd developed a taste for it during the Dust Bowl and never returned thereafter to polite society, except once a year when he visited on Christmas, showing up like clockwork that morning, dusty but clean-smelling, bearing strange gifts and strange stories. It was from Albert, sitting up late by the fire on Christmas night, that Byron first heard about the great road legends, Lefty McClain, Jailbird Jackson, stories that were still passed on today, and it was in those stories that he'd first glimpsed certain skulking possibilities—for freedom and adventure, yes, but also infamy, even immortality—theretofore obscured by the veneer of domestic life. Later, his uncle had bestowed upon Byron his three fundamental rules, and seeing Albert's phantom there in the orchard, Byron had remembered the first: Never stay in one place too long. And Albert was right: Byron had gotten lazy. He was old and sick and his back ached and he had arthritis in his knee and he lost his breath walking uphill, and that had been a decent place to work, but he'd been there for over a month, and if he was being honest with himself, he knew that some trouble was brewing. And sure enough, that night a fight broke out in the bunkhouse between a new young white who'd just arrived and a big Mexican named Santos and a gun was pulled and fired but by then Byron had slipped out and was already a half-mile down the road, trudging slowly through the moonlight to the next farm, and the shot was so muffled by distance that he might have thought it was a car backfiring if he hadn't known better.

Byron was offered the bottle from his right and took it, swigged deeply, and let the syrupy liquid coat his mouth and throat. Ain't that right, Byron? Red was saying. His voice was gentle but insistent, alerting Byron that he'd missed his cue.

What?

Didn't you travel with him for a while?

Who?

The *Duke*, said Red. The Carjack *Kid*.

So, they'd arrived there already. The others stared at him, waiting in respectful silence. Byron knew what they wanted, what the moment demanded: a story, one of those reverent road parables, shot through with humor, threaded with practical advice, and culminating, ultimately, in a neat, uplifting moral, something they could reflect on later, something that might come in handy in the winter ahead. The year before, he'd recounted the time that he and Corrigan had been doing a hundred in a stolen Porsche when a fat wild turkey had kamikazed them from out of nowhere, and then, as they stood and sadly pondered the mangled bird on the roadside verge, they'd remembered that it was Thanksgiving, and, taking this for the sign it was, they'd stuffed the carcass into a pillowcase and roasted it later that night on a spit in a KOA campsite in Indiana (moral: the universe provides). He could tell that story again, he thought, or he could tell the one about the time Corrigan had been hiding out in St. Louis from a one-eyed loan shark named Ernie "The Swede" Gustafson, who was Norwegian, to whom Corrigan owed a hefty gambling debt, and who carried a snubnosed .38 Special revolver, with which, it was said, he didn't miss. Corrigan had been avoiding Ernie for a week when he was picked up on a B&E and given a nine-month bid in Jefferson City—think of The Duke, Byron would say, lying awake in his cell at night, knowing full well that Ernie would be waiting for him when he got out—during which time Ernie was killed in a freak incident involving a chandelier (moral: the good get lucky. Or: justice prevails).

Byron understood, more than anyone, the importance of that kind of tale: the old stories were what gave their lives a moral—some might say spiritual—weight, and that weight was necessary to balance out, in their low-moment calculations, the long and often burdensome list of things that they had lost, relinquished, or abandoned. But as he pondered which story to offer, Byron's gaze fell on the quiet new kid, who was watching him expectantly from across the circle, his eyes glinting in the firelight, and it felt to him, vaguely but pressingly, that those old yarns were somehow inadequate, and that spinning them out now would do a disservice, though to whom he couldn't quite say. What he wanted to tell them about instead was the summer, decades earlier, when he and Kid Kansas had boosted a funeral-black Cadillac straight off the lot in Iowa City and driven it across Wisconsin and the long, lonely Upper Peninsula and then—how had they gotten past Customs?—into Canada, where they'd pitched west, skirting the edge of Lake Superior, and then driven through Manitoba and up into Saskatchewan, whose endless, golden wheatlands Byron could see in his mind, radiant beneath the carbon-paper sky. But that story didn't quite fit the mold: the moral, if there was one, was vague—just the look of those fields in the sun, he thought—and it offered nothing practical—how *had* they gotten past Customs?—and so Byron said, Yeah, we travelled together some, and then pulled a heavy gob of phlegm from deep inside his ruined lungs and deposited it into the dirt before him.

Another pause, until it was clear that Byron was not going to say more, and then the talk gathered again and Byron took a breath. The air was full of the chlorine vapor emanating from the plastics factory and the smell of weeds and axle grease from the yard and the malodorous smoke from whatever they'd found to burn. He looked again at the new kid, who was smiling now at whatever old story they'd moved on to—a wry smile, he thought, affected, performative of knowingness, of world-wisdom, but he wasn't fooling anyone—and there, at the edge of the circle, Corrigan's figure blinked into form again, standing just over the kid's shoulder. This time, he seemed to be looking at Byron— face clean-shaven as he'd always kept it, familiar bandana tied around his neck, huge hands hanging at his sides— and Byron was tempted, for a moment, to speak to him, say his name. But in the next instant a hoot of laughter rose up from the men around the fire and the figure flickered out again. The laughter continued and Byron thought of all the stories that might have just punchlined, all the old, glorifying legends—all of them at least half fabrication, he thought, and some wholly invented—and it felt to him, not for the first time but in a new and urgent way, that those stories disguised something, some essential, lurking truth, some lesson which it seemed suddenly necessary to impart to this poor, lost kid, who in the firelight seemed to glow with innocence. And so, before the laughter had dissipated, Byron said, in a too-loud voice, I'll tell you a story about Kid Kansas.

He'd broken their rhythm, interjected out of order. The laughter snuffed prematurely. If it had been someone else, someone of lower stature, they might have rolled right over him and on to the next story, the next point on the map, but because it was Byron, they gulped their laughter back down their throats and held it.

Sure, Byron, Black Tony said after a moment. Go ahead. Tell us about the Kid.

Byron waited until the air was fully charged, until the new kid leaned forward on his crate, then began: Man had hands like porterhouses. If he made a fist, they resembled Christmas hams. You wouldn't think of a thick-fingered man like that as dexterous, but I swear on the grave of my dear, departed mother that Corrigan could hotwire a car faster than you can tie your boot. It was a thing to see, and I saw it many times, like watching a magician twist a poodle out of a balloon. It gave you a certain feeling, watching, a tightening in your gut, like witnessing a rite from a lost religion, and then the engine sparked to life and you were flying, gone.

He had them now, he knew, and so he paused again, taking his time. He reached for the bottle and was obliged.

One night, he went on, the night I want to tell you about, we'd been squatting in a warehouse in Denver. This must have been the winter of seventy-eight, seventy-nine, and the city had mostly cleared out for the season, but The Duke and I had a good operation going, boosting old Civics and Corollas and selling them to the scrapyard for parts—a good way to make a couple hundred, boys, if you're ever hard up—and so we'd been hanging around, toughing it out. But there'd been a cold snap, and we were freezing our balls off in this big drafty warehouse, and the money was drying up, anyway, so we decided to vamoose. We were all packed up and ready to go. Only question was, where? The Kid favored the Texas coast—there was a girl down there he wanted to check in on—and I favored Arizona, where I knew a guy in landscaping who'd give us work, and we were discussing these possibilities as we walked out of the liquor store, when a lipstick-red Corvette pulls up to the curb, and this old schmuck gets out—you know the type: hair plugs, tropical shirt, dark shades even after the sun's gone down—and he flashes a smug little smile as he brushes past us into the liquor store, and the Kid and I exchange a smug little smile of our own—because how often does this kind of cosmic gift come along?—and by the time the schmuck has paid for his Piña Colada mix, we're on the highway, heading west.

That car: Byron could still feel the muscle of it, the low growl. It ate up the road. The schmuck must have just stopped for gas because the tank was full. They drove until the city lights were just a dim haze in the rearview mirror and the stars spread out before them—the night was moonless, Byron remembered but didn't say, and the stars were so close and brilliant that it seemed like they were driving out into them—and the road unfurled beneath them as they drove, with no thought to their destination, because it was clear that the universe had taken over—here, on cue, a low, cynical groan exhaled from his audience, prompting Byron to raise a finger and say, No, no, I mean it, our fate was out of our hands—and they crossed the flat eastern plains of Colorado—not talking much, he remembered, just passing the hooch back and forth, listening to the engine—and those roads are meant for driving, flat and open and straight as a cue stick. They must have crossed the state line in the dark, but Byron wasn't thinking about where they were, because at some point—he remembered but didn't say—he'd begun to feel that they were not covering distance, really, not moving through space at all, but through some other, older medium, and Byron was about to say something about it to Corrigan—what could he have said?—when The Kid said, Hey, I know this road.

What's out here? Byron said, spooked, but Corrigan didn't answer right away. He'd slowed down and was squinting through the windshield, as though he could see something beyond the circumscription of empty winter fields illuminated by the headlights, and then he came to a junction: one of those county roads without a name, County Road X or County Road Y. He slowed down even more as he made the turn, and said, again, under his breath, I know this road. They passed a sign that said, Welcome to the Town of Woods, Kansas (Unincorporated), and Corrigan switched the headlights off and the true deep gloom of the night appeared before them—impermeable, endless—and the Corvette finally slowed to a stop in the road, and Byron peered out the window, searching the blackness for a town, but there was no town, there was only darkness and, above, the wheeling maelstrom of stars.

Corrigan was looking out the window, too, and Byron knew better than to speak and break the tension that had built up in the car like a seeping gas, and was still building, so that his mouth went dry and his breath became tight. Then, just as some blocky forms began to gather themselves out of the blackness outside, a square of yellow light appeared, just a few short paces from the road. Byron gasped, but Corrigan seemed utterly unsurprised, as though he'd been waiting for that light to ignite, had sparked it somehow with his will: a window, Byron realized, through which, after blinking a few times, he could see patterned wallpaper and a low wooden table, where a bowl of fruit and a greasy hunk of metal rested on a page of newspaper. A kitchen. Somebody's home.

Byron looked at Corrigan but Corrigan stared at the window as though waiting for something else to happen, and a heartbeat later, a figure stepped into the light—a woman, somewhat advanced in age, face lined by worry or hardship, white hair frizzed like a halo around her head— and looked out at them. Forgetting momentarily that they were invisible in the darkness, Byron's impulse was to hide, slink down in his seat, or else to bolt, but Kid Kansas never moved, and indeed seemed to have stopped breathing entirely. He stared intently at the woman in the window, who stared back, unblinking.

Finally, after what seemed like many minutes, the woman moved away and the kitchen light was extinguished and in its place another light was lit, a bright porch light that glowed round and white like a false moon and better illuminated the town of Woods, Kansas—which was, Byron saw now, not really a town: it was just a few buildings, three or four old houses and a barn—and illuminated, also, the face of The Carjack Kid, on which shone the wet tracks of fresh tears.

That was his house, wasn't it? interrupted a voice in the railyard, and though he was looking at the ground and had never heard the voice before, Byron knew whose voice it was. That was his mother?

Byron looked up at the kid and nodded sadly. For though they'd never spoken of it, not that night—after Corrigan had finally remembered the gas pedal and they'd driven in silence across the Panhandle and the lonely plains of Texas and kept driving after dawn broke pale and cold outside of Abilene until they reached the bright, warm coast, where Corrigan had wandered off to find his girl and Byron had found a quiet spot on the beach and watched the tide come in—and not in all the rest of their long time on the road together, either, Byron had understood that experience as some kind of awful journey into Corrigan's past, which had stayed fixed, static, suspended in time. Or else—since The Kid had told him previously that his mother was dead, run off the road by a semi—they'd travelled together into the afterlife, where his mother, aged, was waiting for him. Or else Corrigan had lied about his mother dying and they had simply, through the bewildering magic of destiny, ended up at his house. Or perhaps that wasn't his house, at all, and someone else's mother had stared out at the dark corner of the world they'd happened to occupy at that moment. Truth was, Byron didn't understand exactly what had happened, but when he closed his eyes he could still see that woman's face staring back at him through the window, as grand and inscrutable as fate.

The men gathered around the fire let out a long collective sigh, and then a silence descended: the kind of silence that traps you, pins you down and won't let up. They were all thinking, no doubt, of their own mothers, their own abandoned homes. For each of them had left someplace behind, and while that place might have receded in memory, condensed itself into a single, dense image—for Byron, it was his father, a life insurance salesman, sitting at the kitchen table in the morning, shining his shoes before leaving for work—it still exerted a kind of power over them, a gravity they were helpless to escape.

Byron looked again at the kid, who seemed close to tears himself, and he felt suddenly depleted, sapped of strength. He rubbed his knee, which had begun to act up: another harbinger of the coming cold. On the breeze now was a new smell—florid, putrescent—blowing off the lake, which was lurking, he knew, in the darkness beyond the factory, invisible but certain, like the cancer growing in his chest.

Finally, Mississippi Jerry broke the silence by saying, Well, Jesus, Byron, thanks for the pep talk, and they all laughed, relieved, and Byron laughed, too, and the bottle made its circuit and was exhausted and a new bottle produced, and after a few minutes their gaiety had resumed, though timidly, warily.

Another train churned loudly into the yard and they moved on to the phase of the night in which plans were discussed, destinations compared, advice freely given, and the new kid nodded at everything, taking notes in his mind.

How about you, Byron? rasped Murph. You headed for California again this year?

I might be, Byron said, but he could see the future laid out before him: before dawn he'd wake shivering and limp across the dark yard to the tracks. He'd hop the four-forty freight to Chicago, then veer south and head down to Corpus Christi, where'd he'd spend his last winter in the sun. Around him now, the talk went on—before too long, he knew, it would move to women, from whence it would enter the drunk, maudlin phase of the night—but Byron wasn't listening. He was staring into the shifting darkness over the kid's shoulder, because he felt Corrigan amassing there again. He'd appear any moment now, he knew.

Hey, Byron, didn't Kid Kansas end up in Canada somewhere? Red interrupted, disordering the flow of their talk. Byron understood: his story was still weighing on them. It didn't have a satisfactory conclusion, a neat summing-up, and so, in a way, it was still going. Didn't you say he bought a little cabin up there?

Yes, Byron had told them that, last year or the year before, despite the fact that he'd been present at Corrigan's death. How could he have told them about waking up in a freight car next to a body stiff, already cold, already indistinguishable in any way that mattered from the burlap sacks among which they'd bedded down?

The breeze came again off the lake; the air shivered; the figure appeared. But this time, it wasn't Corrigan: it was Uncle Albert, who stood frowning down at him from beneath his hat, ever-cocked at that rakish angle. Byron was surprised. He'd felt The Duke's eyes on him. He'd felt the atmosphere clot, thicken with his guilt. He'd been ready, had Kid Kansas appeared there, to tell them everything: how Corrigan's eyes had been wide open, as if he'd woken in the moment before his death to a vision that stilled his heart; how, looking into those dead eyes, Byron had been seized by a new and awesome fear; how he'd then, without pausing to think about it, dragged The Carjack Kid to the open door of the freight car and flung him out into the wasteland of Nevada; how the thump his body made when it hit the ground had been lost, almost immediately, in the casual clamor of the train.

Yes, if Corrigan had manifested himself again right then, Byron might have told them the real ending to the story. But here instead was Albert, scowling, and Byron could feel the judgement radiating from his uncle's face, the rebuke. Byron had strayed into dangerous territory and, once again, Albert had conjured himself with a warning: the true story about Kid Kansas, he said with his eyes, was not fit to be told.

Byron sighed, summoned a noxious wad of phlegm, and spit. He was older now than Albert ever was, though Albert still knew some things that he didn't. Maybe dying felt like sloughing off a skin. Maybe it felt like homecoming. He'd meet Corrigan soon enough, he knew, and if apologies were due, he'd make them then. Then, the next year, or the year after, or the year after that, in Milwaukee or Toledo or Flint, maybe they'd both be summoned back.

That's right, Byron said slowly, Saskatchewan.

Uncle Albert broke out into his familiar grin and shot Byron a wink, encouraging him. The same Uncle Albert who, that last Christmas at home, when Byron was still young, younger even than the fresh-faced kid across the fire, had sensed his restlessness, seen his fate spread out before him, and before bedding down on the couch for the night, had taken Byron aside and whispered to him a piece of advice: When you leave, don't take nothing with you. No photographs, no souvenirs, no lock of your girlfriend's hair. When you leave home, leave it all behind for good. Advice Byron had followed, and which had served him well.

Any of you boys been up there? Byron went on. Fine country. Big sky, sweet-smelling breeze. Miles of wheat so gold and pretty you want to eat it off the stalk. Yeah, I visited The Duke up there once, years back. He had a nice little spread, worked the land, a few animals in the barn, American baseball on the radio, a pretty plump wife named Eloise who made the best damn meatloaf you've ever tasted, and don't even get me started on her pie.

They were all smiling now. Byron continued: He asked me to stay up there with them and you'll believe me when I tell you that I considered it. I was getting fat and the work was easy and the days were long and warm. But you all know Uncle Albert's first rule, of course.

They groaned happily, relishing this. Above the kid's shoulder, Uncle Albert tipped his hat to Byron and disappeared. The kid was frowning, waiting, and Byron let the pause build.

Who's Uncle Albert? the kid said finally, as Byron had known he would. What rule?

Byron smiled at the him. No matter what troubles the kid had already seen, he had no idea of the ones that awaited him, and that, Byron decided, was for the best.

Albert was my dear old uncle, son, Byron said, a legend among legends, and he taught me everything I know. He had three rules, and they were simple, and you'd do well to listen now and take them to heart: Never stay in one place too long, Travel light and travel alone, and— here the others joined in, too, and their voices formed a merry chorus—wherever it is that you lay your head, that's where you call home.

Summer People

Bright, buzzing summer, and Lorna was watching from the riverbank, sitting in the grass with her legs tucked under and her dress frilled around her in a blue circle. At that place the river bent and as it wound around the turn it slowed and deepened. Behind her the bank sloped steeply up to the parking lot of the American Legion, where flags were waving in the breeze that came down the river. The breeze picked up the smell of the cottonwood sap and the sweetgale that grew along the banks and it riffled through the leaves of the cottonwoods on the other side. The leaves turned and quivered, dark green on top and pale beneath, and Lorna was watching the leaves with the light sieved through them and the boys standing on the other bank.

The boys, her brother Adam and his friend Joe Lloyd, had swum across and now they stood beneath a tall tree that grew close to the water, looking up into its branches and talking. That morning Joe had come over to their house and told Adam about that spot, the tree with the rope swing and the deep place in the middle of the river. As they were leaving, their mother had called out from the kitchen, "Take your sister!" and so Lorna had followed them, as she was used to following Adam, lagging a little way behind, just as she had followed him and his friends in Buffalo before they moved. At home, in private, they were friends. Adam would sometimes pull her from her book and enlist her into his games and schemes, but when he was with his friends there was an unspoken rule that she should keep her distance. That morning she had walked far behind them on the road, alone, and down the grassy path to the river.

On the other bank, Lorna could see that the boys were arguing, but she couldn't hear what it was about. A thick rope hung down from a high limb that grew out over the water, and Joe was holding the end of it in his hand. Then her brother took the rope and wound the end around his arm and began to climb the tree. There were boards nailed into the trunk and Adam climbed them like a ladder, slowly. He climbed until he stood on a lower, thinner branch, the place he would jump from and sail out on the rope's arc over the water. He stood there for a long time, waiting. Lorna could see his legs, but his face was veiled by leaves.

"Come on!" Joe shouted from below.

The breeze blew down again, the leaves moved and sighed, and Lorna knew what was going to happen. There was a change of light, of texture, a taste on the back of her tongue, a shudder to the air. The air, the light, were like the leaves, shivering. She knew it as if it had happened already, she saw it in her mind like a memory, saw Adam float out above the river, saw the rope twist and snap, saw him fall, the awkward fall, his body bowed, that brutal curve, his thrashing limbs. She willed herself to rise, to yell, to throw her body, make it move, but that urge did not come from her body. The urge was in the air, the light, the leaves that shuddered in the breeze.

The breeze died down. Her body blinked and breathed. Adam was still in the tree.

"Adam!" Joe shouted from the bank. "Come on!"

Lorna saw him leave the tree, float out on the rope. She saw it break. She saw his face, surprised, betrayed, suspended in the air above the shallow water near the bank. Not yet far enough out, not over the deep place yet. She saw his face, surprised, not yet afraid.

■ ■

Two weeks after the funeral, Lorna returned to that place on the river. At the entrance to the path, someone had already posted a handwritten sign that said, "No Swimming!" and when she got down to the bank she saw that the rope had been cut down.

Her aunts had gone back to Buffalo; her father had gone back to work. Except for the sign by the river it was as if Adam had passed through a breach in the world that had opened and then closed around him. Opened and closed like the water when it had swallowed him, like the grave they had put him in.

The days after Adam fell had seemed to pass around her, to rush forward quickly while she stood still. The funeral had been small since her family had just moved to Carthage in June for her father's job and they did not know many people yet. A few people from the town had come, their neighbors, some men who worked with her father at the water treatment plant and their wives. The women had all cried, Lorna's mother and her aunts and the others. Her father and the men had stood stone-faced, lowered their eyes away from the crying. Lorna had not cried. They had all been waiting for her cry, but she hadn't, not at the funeral, or afterwards, or before. Not when she told the police officers what had happened, how Adam had fallen into the shallow water near the bank and not come up, how Joe Lloyd had run out to the road for help, screaming, and two men had come back with him and found Lorna standing in the water to her waist, waiting, cold. Not when they picked her up and carried her back to the bank, put a blanket around her and took her away.

Lorna sat down on the bank again. There was no breeze now and the air was dense and heavy. The river drifted around its curve, passed by. In the high sun Lorna could see that the water held a greasy sheen, the light swirled on the surface. There was the place, the spot he had entered and not come up. They had told her that he had broken his back when he landed in the shallow water, that a boy could drown in shallow water if his back was broken. They had taken him out of the water, she knew, put him in a coffin and put him in a grave. But she had not seen them take him out. She had seen him fall, disappear, and not come up. She had waded out into the river and stood there, waiting.

She was waiting now, again. She had wanted to get out of the house, away from her mother, who each morning seemed more and more delicate, so that Lorna had become afraid to touch her, look at her, as though she might through look or touch dissolve her mother's brittle bones.

But now she knew that she was waiting again, or had never stopped. For the breach to open up again.

She heard footsteps on the path behind her. She turned and saw the girl emerge into the place where the bushes opened up onto the bank.

The girl was wearing shorts and a yellow shirt. She was not wearing shoes. She walked down the bank and stood next to Lorna. She was bigger than Lorna, but Lorna was small for her age. They stood looking at each other for several seconds. The girl had very curly brown hair, cut short around her face. Her face looked friendly, curious, but she was not smiling. Then she said, "You're the girl whose brother died."

It was not a question, but Lorna said, "Yes." Somehow it felt good to hear it put that way. It made her feel more solid, real. She was the girl whose brother died.

The girl nodded and looked at the other bank. Her nose was sprayed with freckles. "My grandma says she's been telling them to cut down that rope for years."

"It was Joe Lloyd's fault," Lorna said, a thought which had not occurred to her until it came out of her mouth.

The girl shook her head and said, "No," but not reproachfully. She seemed to think for a moment, then said, "Maybe it was the rope's fault for breaking."

"I saw it," Lorna said. "I saw it break."

The girl sat down on the bank next to Lorna and looked across the river at the tree. They were quiet for a while, looking. Then she said, "What's your name?"

The girl's name was Janine. She was ten, she said, a year older than Lorna. When Lorna told her that they had just moved there from Buffalo, Janine's face broke into a wide smile, and Lorna noticed that one of her front teeth was chipped.

"I've been to Buffalo," she said. "My dad took me."

Then, from behind them, a man's voice called, "Janine! Janine!" The voice came from the parking lot of the American Legion.

"That's my dad," Janine said. "I have to go now."

Lorna almost told her to wait, but Janine had already risen to her feet. Lorna watched her run to the entrance of the path, watched her bare feet. Just before she was out of sight, Janine turned and shouted back, "I'll come by your house tomorrow!" Then she vanished back into the bushes along the path and Lorna was alone again by the river.

■■

The next day Lorna's mother wanted to take her to the doctor for her checkup, but Lorna begged and her mother relented. She waited for Janine all morning, sitting on the front porch and reading. She read a few lines at a time and then lifted her eyes to the street, waiting. Janine never came.

She let her mother take her to the doctor the day after. She let herself be weighed and measured, let the doctor listen to her chest and thump her back lightly with his knuckle. She breathed in and out. The doctor had a mustache and thick, bushy eyebrows. At the end he told a joke about a pig. Lorna knew he was trying to make her laugh, to see if she would laugh. She laughed.

When they got home, Janine was on the porch, sitting where Lorna had sat waiting the day before. A red bicycle was leaning up against the maple tree in the yard.

"I'm sorry I didn't come yesterday," she said. "I forgot to ask you where you lived! But this morning I thought to ask Mr. Hendricks at the post office, and he told me."

Janine turned to Lorna's mother, who was standing there, frowning, confused. "Hello, ma'am," Janine said. "My name is Janine McDonough." Janine stood up straight and stuck her hand out stiffly.

The gesture was so oddly formal that it made Lorna's mother hesitate for a moment. Then she laughed abruptly, and the sound of her laugh cut through Lorna, she heard it in her teeth. Her mother shook Janine's hand and said, "Very nice to meet you."

"Do you want to come over to my house?" Janine asked Lorna. "My grandma said she would take us to pick blueberries. She knows all the best spots."

Lorna looked up at her mother, who was frowning again. A familiar worried wrinkle had emerged between her eyes.

"I live just across town," Janine said. "I can write my phone number down for you if you'd like."

■ ■

Janine's house was at the end of a steep dirt road, set back in the woods. They left their bikes outside. A small white dog started barking loudly when they went in the door until Janine said, "Oh shut up, Reggie," and the dog wagged its tail furiously and licked Lorna's leg. Inside, it was cool and dim. The trees blocked the sun and the light that came in was shadowed green from the leaves. It smelled like grease and baking and something else, a sweet smell that Lorna didn't know.

In the kitchen, Janine's grandmother was kneeling on the floor, scrubbing the linoleum with a sponge. "Hi, Grandma," Janine said.

Her grandmother looked up. She had the same short, curly hair as Janine, fully white. "Hi, sweetheart," she said. "Stay out of here, now, don't mess up my floor."

They walked around through the living room onto the back porch, which looked out onto a cleared yard and garden and the woods beyond. A man was sitting in a rocking chair on the porch, reading a newspaper. He was smoking a pipe, and Lorna realized that the other smell in the house was smoke.

"Daddy, this is Lorna Seaman," Janine said.

Her father looked up from his newspaper, and then folded it carefully and stood up. He was handsome, he had broad shoulders and a long, square face and close-cropped hair. He was wearing reading glasses with thin metal frames. He extended his hand to Lorna in exactly the same manner that Janine had adopted with Lorna's mother. Lorna shook it.

"Lorna, it's a pleasure to meet you. I'm Jack McDonough." He sat down again and said, "What are you girls into today?"

"Blueberries with Grandma," Janine said.

Her father nodded and smiled. "Well, don't let your grandmother eat them all before you get home." Then he looked at Lorna. "I was very sorry to hear about your brother, Lorna. It's very sad."

Lorna did not know what to say, but she saw a real sadness in his eyes. But it wasn't pity, which is what she had seen in the eyes of other adults. His sadness was different, and Lorna recognized that he didn't expect her to say anything, that he wanted nothing back.

"Come on," Janine said. "Let's go to my room until Grandma finishes cleaning."

In her room Janine had taped dozens of pictures on the walls. They were strange, they were not of movies or bands she liked or sports teams, they were of green pastures and beaches lined with colorful buildings and boats and people sitting at tables outside on a city street. Lorna recognized the Eiffel Tower in one picture above Janine's desk.

"I love France," Janine said. "Have you been to France?"

"No," Lorna said, "but I've been to Canada."

"Me too, but not France. My mom and dad have been there, though. Daddy's been three times. He's going to take me when I'm older."

"Do you speak French?"

"Un petit peu," Janine said. "That means, 'a little bit.' I get to start taking it in school next year."

On her desk was a photograph in a wooden frame of a man in an Army uniform, standing in front of a house. He looked like Janine's father but younger, same long face and dark eyes.

"Is that your dad?" Lorna asked.

"That's my grandpa," Janine said. "He died before I was born, when my dad was just little. He was killed in

France, shot down in a plane. This one here is my dad." She pointed to another framed photograph on her dresser. Her father was wearing a uniform, too, but it was different, no helmet, and he seemed to be standing in a jungle, which reminded her of images she had seen on television.

"Is he in Vietnam?" she asked.

Janine nodded solemnly. "He's going back. He's on furlough now."

Lorna leaned in to look at the photograph. Janine's father was smiling. Lorna liked something in his face, a firmness that was not in her own father's face, which pouched and sagged. An assurance, an easy confidence.

They spent the afternoon out in the woods with Janine's grandmother. There were no trails but Janine's grandmother led them across clear, narrow streams and through dense thickets of chokeberries and bittersweet and buttonbush. Her grandmother carried a cane but used it only to push through the undergrowth. They found three separate patches of berries. When they had filled their pails from the first patch, the three of them sat next to a rocky creek and ate them and drank iced tea Janine's grandmother had brought in a thermos. When they were done their mouths and hands were stained purple and they washed off in the creek. Even Janine's grandmother knelt and put her face in the water. The water was cold in Lorna's mouth. She drank and drank and came up gasping.

They filled their pails again in the next two patches, singing songs that Janine and her grandmother taught Lorna, and they carried the berries back to the house. It was late afternoon when they got back. Janine's mother was at home now, making dinner. When they walked in with the berries, she laughed and said, "I guess we're having pie for supper."

She invited Lorna to stay for dinner but Lorna said that her mother was expecting her at home. She knew she could have called, but she felt the need for them to understand that her mother was waiting for her, that she had her own place to go. Janine's mother emptied one pail of berries into a canvas sack for Lorna to carry, and Janine rode with her back to her house. In the yard, she said, "Tomorrow Mom needs me to help her at work, but I'll come over on Saturday."

Lorna's mother was sitting in the living room when she came in. She had a white washcloth laid over her forehead. When Lorna showed her the blueberries, she smiled weakly and said, "Good work, honey. Why don't you put them in the sink so they don't leak? We can make muffins tomorrow."

That night Lorna's father brought home pizza. Lorna's mother didn't eat, she said she had a headache and went to bed early. Lorna watched television with her father until he fell asleep in his chair. The next day, her mother's head still hurt, and Lorna spent the day reading in front of the television and eating cereal. By evening the blueberries had gotten soft and bled purple through the bag. Lorna ate a few handfuls of the pulpy mash and threw the rest away.

■ ■

Janine's mother worked cleaning houses for the people who came up to Carthage for the summer, and some days Janine had to go with her to help. On the other days, she showed up at Lorna's house in the morning. If Lorna's mother was having a bad day, Lorna would wait for her outside on the porch.

Janine was different than anyone Lorna had ever known. Lorna was bookish and shy, and her friends in Buffalo had mostly been that way, too. She avoided the children who were loud, who were afraid of silence, who seemed to feel a need to test every seam of the world with their voices and bodies, to see which ones would not hold. Janine was loud and forceful, but Lorna wasn't. Janine was solid, constant. She did not waver. Lorna saw this quality in some adults, but not all of them. Not her mother. Adam had been the only other child that Lorna had known like that.

On some of those remaining days of summer, they rode their bikes out to Lake Abanakee, which was a mile from town on the state highway. The lake was long and narrow, and along the near shore there were big houses with decks and high glass windows looking out over the water, the houses that Janine's mother cleaned. There was a marina on the shore, with three long docks jutting out into the water and boats tied to both sides, bobbing in the small waves. Janine knew the owner of the marina, a friendly French Canadian named Jacques. Janine would ask him if he had any work that they could do, and he always found some small job for them, hosing off the rental boats or clearing weeds from the side of the road that led to the boat launch or cleaning the windows of the office. The marina was busy, there were always people moving up and down the docks, and when they were done working and Jacques had paid them a dollar each, they would sit and watch them, young tan couples in white outfits, tying and untying their new speedboats and sailboats. They reminded Lorna of the Kennedys. Janine called them summer people.

On other days they went to the beach to swim, or to a secret place that Janine knew, at the end of a narrow path off the highway. It was a small, rocky cove, and where the lake curved into it there were three large boulders that rose steeply from the water. The largest boulder, Janine told Lorna the first time she took her there, was called Indian Rock. "People say there didn't used to be a lake here, and there was an Indian who got trapped underneath the rock somehow and died," she said. "Then the rest of the Indians cried so much that their tears made the lake."

They walked out to the edge of the rock and looked down into the water.

"It's deep," Janine said, looking at Lorna. "It's safe. Watch, I'll go first."

But Lorna did not feel afraid when she was with Janine. Before Janine could move, she backed up three steps, ran forward, and flung herself off the rock. She did not look down as she fell, she looked up at the sky, which was very clear and blue. She watched it until the lake came up and took her. Then she stayed underwater for a long time, still looking up at the wavering brightness, until she heard another splash nearby and kicked her way back to the surface, where Janine's head was already bobbing, smiling.

■■

School started in September. Although Lorna was in the fourth grade and Janine was in the fifth, all of the grades were in the same large, brick building, and Lorna saw Janine at recess, in the cafeteria at lunch, and in PE class, which was mixed between the fourth, fifth, and sixth grades. Adam would have been in seventh grade, and Lorna watched the boys in that year, imagined him sitting with them at lunch or out on the front steps, where they congregated after school. She often saw Joe Lloyd, but he never said anything to her and looked away if their eyes ever met.

Lorna had always been good in school. Adam, who had never been very interested in it, had mocked her for reading so much, had sometimes called her "the brain," in a nasal accent that was supposed to be Russian, an evil scientist, something he had seen on television.

Adam had struggled with reading, but for Lorna it was fluent, effortless. When she read, she played a game with herself: if a page ended in the middle of a sentence, she would pause before turning it and guess what the next word would be. That year, school seemed to require less from her than ever before, though she knew it was supposed to be getting harder. The answers presented themselves to her, they were floating in her head, she could pluck them out like fruit, like cottonwood seeds from the air.

On the playground one day in October, Lorna was sitting with Janine on the bleachers by the baseball field when a boy came up to them. He was in Lorna's class. His name was Collin Spears. He was skinny with hair that fell evenly all around his head, as if his mother had cut it with a bowl. He said, "Hi, Lorna," with a sneer. "You look very ubiquitous today."

This was a quiet joke in Lorna's class. The week before, her class had been assigned to write a short essay about local plants or wildlife. Lorna had written about birds, and the day after she turned her essay in, her teacher, Mrs. McConnell, had asked her to stand up and read it out loud. The essay contained the line, "In spring and summer, the red-breasted robin is ubiquitous in this area." The class sniggered, and Lorna understood that they thought she was showing off. Her use of such a word, especially in a sentence that also contained the word "breasted," had set her apart, and when Mrs. McConnell, beaming, told her to sit down, Lorna had waded back to her desk with her head down. Since then, she had heard the other students saying the word to each other, imitating her. Now, on the playground, Lorna was conscious of a group of boys behind her. She could not see them but she could feel them there. Collin Spears was their emissary and they were waiting for what would happen to him.

What happened was that Janine stood up from the bleachers and reached her hand across the gap between them and slapped Collin Spears on the cheek. The sound vibrated in the air, the fleshy clap. The boy looked shocked. His eyes grew wet as he stood there with his mouth open. Then he turned and walked away, quickly, Lorna knew, before he started crying. As he rounded the bleachers on the way back to the other boys, he said, "You bitch."

Janine sat back down beside her. "Idiots," she said. "What did he call you?"

"Ubiquitous," Lorna said softly. "It means common, easy to find."

Janine frowned. "Oh," she said.

■ ■

In early November, Janine's father went back to Vietnam. After school on most days, Lorna went back to Janine's house and they did their homework together at the dining room table. The house had changed, an emptiness had grown there and hung in the rooms, dense and quiet, mixing with the smell of pipe tobacco which lingered, fading. Usually, Janine's mother was out, and her grandmother was watching the old movie channel on the small television in her room. Still, Lorna preferred Janine's house to her own, with its different kind of absence. Because they had only lived there for a month before he died, Adam's room was mostly bare and there were no traces of him in the other rooms, no residues of his existence there.

Lorna helped Janine with her homework, especially her French and English. Lorna had never taken French before, but she picked it up from Janine's books and worksheets and a pocket dictionary that was in the house. Janine could not keep straight her verb tenses and noun genders, and when she had finished her work Lorna would look it over and correct her mistakes. Nearly every day, Janine wrote a letter to her father. To save on postage, she would save them up for a week before she sent them, all together. At the dining room table, Janine wrote page after page in her thick-ruled notebook.

"What do you write to him about?" Lorna asked one afternoon.

"Just anything," Janine said. "Like what happened at school, or whatever's going on in town. Now I'm telling him about Jamie Watkins's deer."

Walking back from school that day, they had encountered a small group of people on Main Street, crowded around Jamie Watkins's truck. In the truck bed was a deer, a buck with big branching antlers. The tailgate was open and the buck's head lolled over the edge.

"Do you ever write about me?" Lorna asked.

"Sometimes."

"What do you say?"

Janine smiled and said, "I say that you're the smartest person in the school and that you're going to be President."

She went back to writing, and Lorna tried to imagine Janine's father getting those letters, where he was. She had seen it on the news, watching with her own father. Helicopters landing in high grass, men wading through shallow water, explosions in the sky, men sitting along a riverbank, muddy, smoking. Her mother couldn't watch; she left the room. Most nights they showed pictures of soldiers who had been killed. They were smooth-faced, smiling boys, much younger than Janine's father, who was an officer. Lorna knew that seeing them made her mother think of Adam.

Her father watched. He shook his head. He seemed to be against the war, but he seemed to be against everything.

He said, "All those guys over there, getting blown up. We should just nuke the whole damn country and be done with it."

■■

Lorna's aunts came to visit for Thanksgiving. They were kind, lonely women, and they talked about Adam, told stories about him when he was a baby, tried to fill the house with him, until it became clear that it upset Lorna's mother. Usually, they never spoke of him in their house. When her aunts talked about him, Lorna remembered the day by the river. She heard the shimmering leaves, she felt the breach behind the air, beneath her skin.

Janine had the idea about the houses not long after that. The summer people were gone, and the town felt oddly vacant without them, a different town altogether. Janine's mother had taken a waitressing job at the Oak Barrel, but she still had the keys to those houses by the lake. They hung on the wall of Janine's living room, each on a separate peg below a piece of masking tape with the owner's last name written on it. Janine had been in the houses, helping her mother clean. "They're just sitting empty," she told Lorna. "No one's going to use them until spring."

The next afternoon, they rode their bikes out to the lake, just as they had in summer. There was snow on the ground. They rode past the path that led to Indian Rock and up the hill until they came to the first house, the Johnsons', where they turned off onto the steep driveway that led to the water. The house was large, split-level with a steeply pitched roof and big windows that looked out on the lake. They stood at the doorway for a moment, and then Janine knocked, though the house was clearly empty. Then she took the key from her pocket and opened the door.

Inside, the house was dim and dusty, the big front windows veiled with thick curtains, and they opened the curtains and turned on all the lights and stood in the living room, waiting for the house to come alive. Then they went through the rooms, one by one. They turned all the faucets, but the water had been turned off for the winter. They opened the refrigerator and found it empty and dark. In the bedrooms, they opened the closets. The house was cleaned out, the hangers hung empty, a particular kind of emptiness, both familiar and strange.

Over the next two weeks, they visited all of the houses that had keys, never going to more than one a day, as a rule, since it seemed too brash to leave more than one key peg empty at a time. In some of the houses, they found things that had been left, forgotten. They found a raincoat hanging by itself in a closet. They found a stuffed pig under a bed in a child's room. In a drawer they found several yellow pages on which someone had written what Lorna thought was the beginning of a novel about a boat trip down the Amazon. On a bed they found a pair of woman's underwear, as small and red as a popped balloon, so delicate that the girls felt nervous to touch it. They found matchbooks and half-empty packs of cigarettes, jars of peanut butter and jam in cupboards, discarded magazines spread over the arms of couches, a man's toupée draped over a lampshade like the carcass of a small, car-flattened animal.

Lorna tried to imagine the people whose things they were, the people she had seen at the marina in August, those sleek, tan, thin-eyed people. In the photographs on the walls men held up dangling fish, women lounged on deck chairs in sun hats, children played in the sand at the beach. The things did not add up to an entire life. They were remnants, fragments, but handling them Lorna could sometimes feel the ghostly remainders hovering in the house, the way that in midsummer she would sometimes catch a smell on the breeze, something cool and crisp that came from sleeping winter.

■■

Just before school let out for winter vacation a blizzard fell overnight and covered the town, and the next day Janine's mother decided to take them sledding before she went to work. In the morning they crowded into the car, Lorna, Janine, Janine's mother, and Janine's grandmother, and drove to the golf course on the far edge of town. The course was closed and buried and they dragged the sleds through the snow to the top of a long, steep hill. Janine's grandmother stayed in the car with the engine running, listening to the radio, and the three of them took turns going down and then trudging back up to the top, again and again. Then they went two at a time, racing, and then all three together on their separate sleds, shouting over the snow.

Lorna watched Janine's mother. She flew down the hill much faster than the girls, because she was heavier but also, Lorna thought, because she seemed to want it more.

She leaned forward in the sled, thrust her head forward like a speed-skater. She ran back up the hill, yelling, "Faster, faster," cheeks flushed, eyes bright.

Janine's father's letters, when they came every few weeks, had been full of small, cultural details and exhortations to work hard in school. Often, he had included, "Say hello to Lorna." Watching Janine's mother on the sled, Lorna understood that this, her strange giddiness, her desire for speed—"Faster, faster"—had to do with waiting, too, that they were all, all three of them, waiting for something to happen, or return. But nothing was happening. Nothing was changing. The scenes of their lives were moving forward while they watched, motionless, from the riverbank.

When they were tired and cold, they walked back to the car, where Janine's grandmother had fallen asleep. She startled awake as they were driving past Ned Bennett's farm. Out the window they could see the house and the barn and the covered hay chute that sloped down into the snow from the top of the barn.

"When I was a girl, we had a hay chute just like that one," Janine's grandmother said. "There was a little room at the bottom where the hay would collect, just big enough to stand up in when it was empty. It had a glass window that our father would take off when he wanted to get hay out for the cows. Most of the year it was full of hay, but in the summer, the cows ate grass, and then it was empty and we would climb up into the barn and slide down the chute. When we got to the bottom we climbed out the window and went back up."

Lorna and Janine turned and watched the barn fade in the window behind them. Janine's grandmother went on from the front seat.

"One day, I guess my father had put the window back on, and we climbed up in the barn without checking it. I slid down first and when I got to the bottom I saw that the window was closed. I don't know why, but I panicked. I could have yelled back up the chute to my brothers to go down and open the window, but somehow I didn't think of that. I thought I was trapped down there. The only thing I could think to do was take off my shoe and throw it at the window, and when it broke I climbed out and cut myself deep on the leg."

Lorna could see the old woman's face, staring out the windshield at the snow.

"My mother was angry that I cut myself and my father was mad because of the window," she said. "They asked why I didn't just call for help, or try to climb back up the chute, but I couldn't explain it. I still can't explain it. I was trapped in there. I just had to get out. I couldn't breathe or think. I was trapped."

■ ■

In one of the empty houses on the lake they found an entire dresser full of clothes, which Janine found scandalous, extravagant. "One whole set of clothes just for this house, just for a few weekends when they're here," she said.

"Isn't it worse to have the house at all?" Lorna said. "An extra house?"

Janine laughed. "An extra house! It is worse! Summer people!"

They took the clothes from the dresser and put them on. Lorna put on a yellow sundress over her sweater and pants, the shoulder straps so long that the neckline hung to her belly and the hem swept along the floor. Janine took off her clothes and put on a white button-down shirt and khaki pants that she rolled above her ankles. They stood next to one another in front of the full-length mirror on the bathroom door.

"Quelle belle êtes-vous, Madame!" Janine said. "Enchanté."

"Tout le plaisir est pour moi, Monsieur," Lorna said.

They took the clothes off and put them carefully away. Then Janine lay down on the big bed and Lorna climbed up next to her. They lay on their backs, looking up at the high, exposed beams of the ceiling.

Janine turned her face to Lorna. She said, "I'm sorry I never met your brother."

Lorna looked back at her, her round face framed by her thick, curly hair. Janine's face was not perfectly even, it was lopsided, one eye very slightly lower than the other.

Her whole life, Lorna had felt like a person still coming into form, not as solid as other people seemed to feel. Here was her body, but her self was diffuse, porous. The world came in and out like a breeze through a house with the windows open. Janine was not like that. Janine was dense, sound. Adam had been that way, too.

"I saw it," Lorna said. "When he died . . ."

She wanted to tell Janine about the leaves, the breeze, that day by the river. That she had known what would happen. That she had done nothing. But Janine said, "I know. I know you saw," and Lorna didn't say anything else. She felt a kind of gathering, felt the tears rise behind her face, and she turned away onto her side. She had never cried about Adam. She had seen him fall, disappear, and not come up. She had waded out into the river and stood there, waiting. Somehow, she had not believed, still did not believe, that he would not come up.

Lorna was facing the big windows that looked onto the lake, and through them she could see the hills and bare white trees on the far shore. From that angle she could not see the lake below but she could feel it there, the cold dark water that would soon stiffen, shiver into glass.

■ ■

For Christmas Lorna's family drove back to Buffalo and stayed with her Aunt Catherine. Her father had to go back to work the next day, but Lorna and her mother stayed for another two weeks. Her mother went for walks with her aunts, and in the afternoon the three of them sat around the living room, drinking tea. Lorna spent her days reading on the carpet in the living room. When she got bored, she wrote short letters to Janine. Janine and her mother and grandmother had taken the train down to North Carolina for Christmas. That was where her mother and father were from, where they had met, where the rest of their families still lived. Lorna did not know the address there, so she addressed her letters to Janine's house in Carthage. She knew that she wouldn't get them until she got back, but it was a way to pass the slow time. In her letters, she used as many French words as she could.

Sometimes, she thought about Adam. There, in her aunt's house, she could remember his face, the small white scar on his left cheek where he had been hit with a hockey puck. She could remember his voice, a nonsense song he had sung sometimes, something about a duck and a kangaroo. It was different to think about Adam in a house that was not their own, in a city where he had known the streets, where the memory of him did not call up the river.

By New Year's Eve Lorna felt restless. Her mother suggested that she call up some of her old friends, but Lorna could not imagine doing that. Those were people from another life. On New Year's Day she left the house and went for a walk by herself through the cold city. As she passed into her old neighborhood, everything was familiar but strange. There was the lot where she and Adam had thrown rocks at each other. There was Mrs. Wagoner's house, where Adam had raked the leaves in the fall. The light was thin and cold, the snow was old and grey and gritty. The city seemed to be suspended, waiting. She felt like a ghost there, no more a part of the world than Adam was now. She walked by their old house and saw that the new owners had cut down the beautiful old maple tree that had been in the front yard. Adam had loved to climb it. He had spent hours in its branches. They had not cut it down all the way, part of the trunk was still there but the branches were gone, and Lorna stood across the street looking at the dead, brown stump, remembering what it had looked like whole and full, in summer.

■ ■

When she got back to her aunt's house, she knew imme-diately that something was wrong. Her mother and Aunt Catherine were sitting at the kitchen table, and Lorna saw on her mother's face that she had been crying. When she came in the door, they both turned to look at her, and she stood in the doorway with her boots and coat on, waiting.

"Oh, sweetie," her mother said. "Oh, sweetie. Come sit down."

Janine's father had been killed. Back in Carthage, Lorna's father had found out somehow and he had called her mother. Lorna listened to her mother say this. Her voice sounded very distant, as though she were speaking underwater. She heard the words, "Janine" and "father" and "killed" and "sorry" but they were like insects buzzing around her face, flitting in and out of view. At some point she was conscious of sitting in her mother's lap while her mother stroked her hair. She was thinking about the day she met Janine, by the river, when she had walked out of the woods on the path by the bank, and spoken, and filled the space that Adam had left behind.

Suddenly, she was seized with urgency. She jumped to her feet.

"We have to go back," she said. "Now. We have to go right now."

"Honey," her mother said, "they aren't at home. They're still away."

"We have to go!" Her voice was raised, almost a shriek. "We have to be there when they get back!"

"Oh, sweetheart," her mother said, her voice breaking, her face streaked with tears. "They aren't coming back."

Lorna blinked, waited.

"Your father said that some men from the base are packing up their house for them. They're going to ship everything down to them. Down to, where are they?"

"I don't know!" she screamed, not in control of her voice. "I don't have the address! I don't know where they are!"

"I'm so sorry, sweetheart," her mother said. "We'll find out where they've gone. You can write her. You can call long distance when we get home."

"Long distance," she repeated. Her voice was flat now. "Gone."

■ ■

When she and her mother got home two days later, there were three letters waiting for her on the kitchen counter. Two were from herself, written to Janine and returned with a yellow note that said, "Recipient no longer at this address." The third was from Janine. There was no return address. Lorna ripped it open and read it in the kitchen.

Dear Lorna,

I'm sure by now you have heard about Dad, and have maybe even tried to reach me. Mom says that the things from our house will get here in a few days, but I don't see where we're going to put it all. We're staying at my Uncle Sam's and even though it is not a small house there isn't much extra room here. Mom's trying to find us a place of our own in town. It's not bad here, though. Uncle Sam has two horses.

The funeral was yesterday, at the Fort. There were two generals there. They shot off the rifles and everything. Grandma said it was "dignified."

Mom says she just can't face the trip back up right now, which I guess is why we had to send for the furniture. I wish I could've said goodbye to you, at least. Mom says that maybe we can come back up to Carthage for the summer. I hope we can.

Uncle Sam gets his mail at the post office in Pittsborough. Mom says that I can get letters there, too, until we find a place. There's no phone here, since we're pretty far out in the country, but we'll have one in town.

You have been a good friend and I love you. Dad liked you too. I'll keep writing to you and I'll let you know what our new address is when we find a place. I will be easy to find. I will be ubiquitous.

Love, Janine

■ ■

Two days later, on her birthday, Lorna went back to the house on the lake where they had put on the summer people's clothes. The house was locked, but she was able to get into the basement through a crawlspace, and then up the stairs into the kitchen. She went back up to the bedroom, slowly, running her hand over the banister, pausing in front of each picture on the wall. In the bedroom she lay down on the bed. It was late afternoon and the light coming in through the windows was feeble, grey. Lorna lay on her back and felt the vacuum of the house. It pressed around her like thick air, a humidity of emptiness.

She lay there for a long time. After a while, she began to cry. It started slowly, but soon it was coming faster and she was gasping, heaving. She cried and cried, as if a spring ran through her, as if her body was made of crying.

She clenched her body and cried until she fell asleep.

She dreamt of summer. She was standing on Indian Rock, alone. She jumped off into the lake and swam down to the bottom, touched the soft dirt there, turned and kicked off the ground up towards the light. But as she got closer to the surface, the light grew dimmer, faded, and then she swam into the bottom and hit her face in the dirt. She turned and saw the light above, kicked towards it again, but again it faded as she got closer, and when she hit the bottom, she understood that she was trapped there. She looked up at the light above the surface. She did not try again. She floated there and watched the light.

When she startled awake it was full night. She lay there, breathing. She filled her lungs with air. She breathed and breathed.

She felt different, now. More solid, stable. Like vapor condensed into water, or water setting into ice. She opened and closed her hands, touched her face, blinked. She could feel her body pressing into the bed, and she felt heavier than before, as if she had acquired new weight.

Outside, she knew, beyond the big windows, the lake was frozen. In the summer, it would melt, then freeze again. The summer people would come back, and leave, and come back, and leave. The years, the days would pass in sequence now, advancing one after the other. Time would just move forward, and she would move forward with it, and the others—Adam, Janine, Janine's father—would be left behind. They would not be coming back.

■ ■

Janine wrote to Lorna twice more, but Lorna did not return any of the letters. It was easier that way, to believe that Janine had only existed while she lived in Carthage, and that now she did not exist at all. It was not all that hard to believe.

Slowly, as the years passed, the soldiers came back to town. Every six months there were a few more of them. Lorna saw them around town, sitting on porches, washing their cars in driveways, crowding around the picnic table at the convenience store. She had not realized that so many of them had been gone, had not felt their absence, but she saw now that the whole town had been waiting for them, and now they had come back. They were everywhere now, young men who walked with their backs straight but bent forward slightly at the waist, as if they were always walking uphill. On her way home in the evenings after basketball practice or drama rehearsal, she sometimes passed the Oak Barrel Tavern, where soldiers drank for half-price. Passing, she could hear their voices, shouting and laughing. They had come back, but somehow it didn't feel like a reunion.

Lorna graduated from high school a year early, when she was seventeen. She had received a scholarship from a good college, not too far away. That last summer, she worked for Jacques at the marina on the lake, as she had every summer since she was fourteen. By now, her French was very good.

One day that July, Lorna was standing on the dock of the marina, chatting with a young woman who had come up from New York. The woman was talking about her son, about where to go for swimming lessons, but Lorna was only half listening. It was a clear, warm day, and a good breeze riled the water and knocked the boats against the docks. The bells on their masts rung out idly.

Then she heard a man's voice, sounding angry, coming from behind her, from the water. She turned and looked. Out on the lake, fifty yards from shore, there was a small sailboat bobbing in the waves. The man was standing at the bow, speaking to a woman, telling her to do something, to trim the jib, maybe, Lorna couldn't hear across that distance. The woman was saying something back, pulling on the sheet.

Then Lorna saw another figure in the boat, a child, a small girl, maybe four or five years old. Blonde hair, blue swimsuit. She was standing at the stern, looking back behind the boat, looking at Lorna, and Lorna felt again the shivering air, the change in the light. The breach was opening up again. She saw the sheet give in the woman's hands, saw the boom swing, saw the boat lurch to port and the girl, unsteady, fall forward into the water. She saw it as she had seen Adam fall, like a memory, as if she had entered a knot in time, and she felt a strange euphoria, standing on the dock. This, she understood, is what she had been waiting for.

She is in the water, now, but she hardly feels it. She is all motion. She hears shouting, but she cannot make out the words or where they came from, from behind her on the dock or from the sailboat ahead. She thinks she hears a child's voice, a scream. She keeps kicking. Her head is down. She is swimming.

The Upper Peninsula

We've had good days, too. One morning I woke to find the light in our bedroom strangely soft and green, shimmering over the walls. I lay in bed and watched it for a while. It reminded me of the surface of a swimming pool. I held my breath, and when I released it, the room began to breathe a little, too. The dust breathed up from the floorboards, lightly. The curtains swelled and slumped. I thought: Yes, this is a different kind of day.

Abe was there, breathing in the bed next to me. We'd both taken the day off work, and he was sleeping in. When the light warmed up and lost its pretty green quality, I watched him instead. He sleeps like a corpse, on his back with his hands crossed over his chest. He's a beautiful sleeper: slack-mouthed, peaceful. Eventually, he lifted one slow eyelid and looked at me.

"Breakfast?" I said.

His eye snapped shut like a little sea creature scared back into its cave.

I got up and walked to the kitchen in my nightgown. Usually, I like to listen to the radio while I cook, but that day I wanted quiet. I wanted to hear what was going on around me. As it turns out, quite a lot goes on. The electric things purred. In the walls, water sloshed through the pipes. In the pan, the bacon spat indecently.

I dropped eggs in the pot to boil. They bobbed around. Abe came up behind me then, drawn by the good smells. He wrapped his arms around my waist and rested his big head on my shoulder. Together, we watched the eggs boil. I could feel them growing firm. I felt something edging in around me, the old heaviness. I'm sorry, I wanted to whisper to the eggs, but I didn't want to disturb the room.

While we ate, we savored the silence. Abe lit a cigarette and I watched the white twist float up into the room. I had an idea. "Let me have some of that," I said. Abe narrowed his eyes at me. I gave it up years ago, but the smoke was just too lovely, rising. "It's a special day," I told him. "The rules don't apply."

He handed me the cigarette and then got up to do the breakfast dishes. On the table were the lilies I'd bought the day before. I looked at them closely while I smoked. I'd put them in a thin glass vase. My thoughts were coming now. The lilies were happy, I thought, floating there, drawing the water up into themselves like I breathed in smoke. They'd been severed from the earth, but they didn't mind. I was starting to feel better.

When he finished the dishes, Abe sat down across from me again. We were in no hurry. We were at our leisure. I held out my hands and he took them. His hands were wet and warm, rough from his work in the foundry. I looked at his face, broad and white and pitted as the moon. At any moment, I could sculpt that face in clay from memory. But that morning, I felt I was understanding something new about him, my husband, who'd shared my bed for many years. It had to do with the quiet that now immersed us. I was steeping in it, like tea, and taking on some of its qualities. Abe was used to that. He doesn't speak anymore. He gave up the use of his voice years ago, when we lost our boy, Jeffrey.

"Are you ready?" I asked him. He gave me his nice, slow smile and nodded.

We got dressed. Abe wore his dark grey suit, which hangs lonely in the closet every other day of the year, cloaked in its plastic shroud. I wore the purple print dress I'd bought the week before on sale. "Zip me up, honey," I said, and he zipped me up. He held out the silver cufflinks I bought him for Christmas years ago, and I did his cuffs.

We went down the back staircase of our apartment building. Abe drove us out onto the streets, and I saw that it was just another normal day in town. People were out, going about their business. The mailman was making his deliveries. The sun was shining fondly over all of it.

We took the old highway out to the coast. That part of the state is farmland, and I knew every farm we drove by. It was like driving into the past. Every now and then Lake Michigan flashed between the trees. We drove with the windows down and I could smell the dirt and the growing things. I pictured the fruit on the branches, still small and hard, but growing. Grow, I told them silently. I was trying something, this silent speaking. Get big and fat and round, I said.

Finally, we reached the turnoff to our farm and Abe turned onto the old dirt road. The trees parted to receive us, and then the fields opened up around us. The fields were all grown over. They were meadows now, the long grass swaying in the breeze. We passed the old barn, nestled in the woods, crumbling, parts of the roof caved in. Our small white house was waiting at the end of the road. It seemed happy to see us as we got out of the car. The paint had peeled, a little more each year. Don't worry, I told the house. Don't be ashamed. It smiled shyly in the sun.

Behind the house, a grassy hill rises up to the crest of the bluff, where an old crabapple tree stands in deep solitude. Beyond, the bluff rolls down to the shore in a gentle, sandy sweep. Abe and I walked up the hill through the grass, which swirled around our knees in the breeze coming off the lake. There used to be a path through the grass. It's all grown over now, but our feet remembered it, and I remembered watching, a hundred times, out the living room window as a boy's bright, floating head traced the path through the grass and then disappeared over the hill as he ran down to the water.

As we approached the tree, I could hear the lake washing over the rocks below, and then it stretched out before us, flickering, green in the shallows and deep blue in the profundities.

The moon was there, pale in the pale sky, half-hidden in her own shadow, hovering above the water. A smattering of friendly clouds floated around her, big as continents but weightless as breath.

For a while, we stood at the edge of the bluff and watched the scene below. Abe closed his eyes. I thought: he's listening, and so I tried to listen, too. It wasn't hard to hear, if you were quiet: the moon was calling sadly to the lake, and the lake, listening, was trying to lift toward it. Let go, I thought. I thought: Once you let go a little, it's easy to go the rest of the way.

Then, for a moment, the world was seized with buoyancy. Everything began to float up towards the moon. The grass stiffened and stretched against its roots. Bees and small white butterflies wafted up out of the grass, where they'd been called from their work among the wildflowers. The flowers lifted their faces and then released their pollen, which hovered in the air, a golden mist. Abe and I rose up on our toes. We lifted our faces like the flowers toward the moon. I held my breath. Let go, I thought again. And for a moment I thought we might. The moon's call was loud and clear, and I thought for once we might all listen. The lake surged and the crumpled roof of the barn thought about righting itself and the crabapple leaves strained against their stems like green hands, waving.

But then a cloud passed over the moon and we all fell back to earth. The leaves and flowers drooped. The pollen caught the breeze and scattered. The lake remembered its great weight and rested again in its bed.

I was crying. "Oh dear," I said aloud. Abe put his arms around me. I rested my face against his chest. We stood there for a while, breathing together. Then he tapped me on the shoulder. His cheeks were wet, too, but he was smiling. He held up his finger and pointed down toward the lake shore. He closed one eye like a painter and slowly swung his arm along, tracing the shoreline with his finger. I sighted down his arm and imagined the coastline as it continued north, beyond where it disappeared into the trees, then wove along into coves and around the headlands out of sight, all the way up to the Mackinac Bridge.

I knew what he was saying. At one time, we used to have a lot of cats running around the farm. They were farm cats, mangy and mean, surviving on the birds and mice. They came and went as they pleased, and made their kittens, and often they would vanish without a trace. It didn't mean anything to us when they disappeared, but Jeffrey couldn't stand it. It seemed like every week he'd come and find me, in the kitchen or the garden, crying because he couldn't find a cat he liked. "But where did she *go?*" he'd ask me, and I don't know where the idea came from, but at some time I started telling him that the cats went on vacation to the Upper Peninsula. That caught on, and after a couple of years he was picturing a whole herd of frolicking animals up there. He was a sweet boy.

I smiled at Abe to show him I understood.

We walked back to the car. As we drove back out to the road, I waved goodbye to our farm. Of course, it isn't ours anymore. It belongs to a bank in New York City. Goodbye, house, I said. Goodbye, lost fields. Goodbye, old wreck of a barn. See you next year.

On the drive home, we turned the radio on. One can have enough of anything, even quiet.

When we got back to the apartment, Reggie was there, waiting for us by the stairwell. "Hello, Reggie," I said. He mewed hello. He's an old cat and he's only got three legs, but he gets around well enough. He stops by sometimes when he gets hungry or lonely. Then he leaves, and we forget about him. He's easy to forget when he's gone.

Inside, I poured him a bowl of milk, which he lapped. As I put the milk away, I noticed the lilies again on the kitchen table. I'd been planning to take them with us to the farm, leave them by the crabapple tree, but now I was glad that I'd forgotten. They looked so nice on the kitchen table, so pretty and bright and hopeful. They were happy there.

I cooked spaghetti for dinner and we ate in front of the television. We just watch whatever's on. Cop shows, game shows: it's all the same to us. But after the gentle quiet of our day, it all seemed so loud, so rude. When I finished eating, I got up to take a bath. I sat on the toilet and waited for the tub to fill up with water while the room filled up with steam. Then I climbed in and let myself float for a while. I was trying not to think, but my thoughts were coming anyway, as loud and rude as the game shows. I wanted quiet, to let go of sound completely. I released my breath and let my head sink beneath the water. Of course, there are sounds underwater, too, but a different sort of sounds. I closed my eyes and tried to listen. I thought: these are the sounds a drowned boy might hear. I'd never had that thought before, and it made me feel better. I was glad to hear them, the swish and hum, a kind of lightness, the muted world. I thought: An ear is nothing but a hole in the head, and a drowned boy has those, too.

When I got out of the bath, Abe was asleep on the couch, head back and mouth open. His cigarette had burned out in the ashtray. The news was on, the war, booms and bangs. I turned off the sound and watched a little. Jeffrey would be there, I thought, if he'd grown up. I knew it, deep inside. All the boys go these days. There are hardly any boys around here anymore.

I turned it off and shook Abe awake. We went to the bedroom and lay down together, facing each other, the way we like to do before sleep. I reach out to touch Abe's face. I traced his jawbone with my finger, feather-light, the way he likes, up his cheek and around his ears, then over his forehead and around his eye sockets. I know that face, every knob and crater. Reggie jumped up and settled in between us, purring. Abe cooed a little, the way he does when he's happy. A pretty, fluttering sound.

"Yes," I told him with every part of me. "It was a good day."

Destiny

I.

Begin at the end, at the beginning of real winter, in the barn, up in the hayloft, alone. In Woods, Kansas, standing in the hayloft door, looking out across the bare December fields. Wrapped in a blanket but still cold, shivering. Quiet, cold, the wind coming in through the long gaps in the walls of the barn. The hayloft door is perhaps thirty feet off the ground and from that height she can see across the fields, across the blank colorless world—it has not yet snowed—to a distant stand of trees. She is looking out at the trees and remembering her dream, in which she was a bird— a long white heron, rising—and lifting her eyes from the fields to the grey sky and remembering that feeling of weightlessness, flight.

Or begin at the beginning, at the end of childhood, in the barn, up in the hayloft, alone. From the hayloft door she can see a bright ocean of gold: her grandfather has a sunflower farm outside of Wichita and the heavy, drooping heads stretch to the limit of her vision. She lowers her eyes from the flowers and looks instead at her doll: cornsilk hair and a red dress. A gift from her mother, who gave the doll to Grace when she left her at the farm before driving off to New York with a self-styled evangelist named Roland. She is singing to the doll, a nonsense song she is making up as she goes, and now she hears a voice calling her name, gently, from below. Her grandmother, calling her for dinner. Calling, Grace? Grace?

II.

She was working on a farm in New York but her coat was thin and when the weather turned she left, flew south. In Charleston, South Carolina, she fell in with a group of other drifters, friendly vagabonds. They slept on the beach or under the boardwalk, made fires from pallets and gnarled skewers of driftwood, ate the fish the fishmongers threw away in the afternoon and the fried things the tourists threw away all the time. They smoked hash if they had it— everything was shared—and drank rum and fortified wine. They stole from people's gardens. It was genial. Arguments were arbitrated. No one bothered them. No one carried a weapon. It was warm in late September. There was always, falling asleep and waking, the sound of the surf.

Eli was one of that group. He had arrived just before she did, coming up from Florida, he said. Selling airboat tours through the Everglades, he told her one night on the beach with the firelight glancing yellow off his forehead. You know, fanboats? Most people come down to see the alligators and the manatees, but I built my reputation on the birds. Cranes, herons, egrets, you'd be surprised how many people come down to see them, and they aren't easy to find. The boat motor scares them off. People leave disappointed. But I had a good sense for them, got to know their favorite places, where their nests were. Rookeries. You should see a heron egg. People are surprised. Small as a chicken egg, hold three in your hand, but blue. Blue, blue like the sky, like a jewel, little miracles. You should see one.

She liked his voice, the rhythm of it, deep and slow. Faintly southern around the edges, but that was acquired, he said. He was from Oregon.

He wore a blue denim jacket lined with red flannel. He walked stiffly, bow-legged, as if he had just dismounted a horse or a motorcycle. He had a large forehead and looked a little like James Cagney (she had watched the old movies with her grandfather when she was a girl). During the day, when the group splintered off into smaller sections, they walked around the city together, like tourists, carrying their backpacks. They sat on the pier and watched the gulls swooping over the harbor. She complained about wanting a hot shower—generally they bathed in the ocean—and he taught her a trick he knew, waiting behind the backdoor of the YMCA until someone came out and then catching the door before it closed.

She had been there two weeks when she woke up one morning and he was gone. She figured that he had moved on, and she wasn't surprised, but she was a little hurt, and the hurt surprised her. She had thought she was beyond that, accustomed to abandonment.

She went back to the Y in the afternoon, turned the water very hot, stood under it for an hour. She wanted to hone the edges of herself. She wanted a new crisp version of herself to emerge, be born, from the blurry background of her life: deliverance. She had three-hundred dollars in a wooden box stuffed deep in her backpack. She was twenty-one years old. She scrubbed herself red, watched the steam rise off her red skin.

Eli came back that night, late, and woke her up by shaking her shoulder. He backed up, motioning for her to follow him. She grabbed her sleeping bag and pack and walked behind him up the beach to the road. Parked on the shoulder was an old Volkswagen Beetle.

Whose car is this? she said.

Mine, he said.

Where are you going?

West, he said. California. Hop in.

She hesitated, looked back down the beach. But it was a perfunctory pause. The air was dense, she felt, with destiny. It was in the breeze and stung her face.

■ ■

The car was not his, and it was full of drugs. One-hundred pounds of crystal methamphetamine, made right here in America, Eli said, and a single pound of black tar heroin (origins unknown). The trunk was full—the spare tire had been taken out—and the backseats had been cut open and filled. Idea is, he said, smiling, don't get pulled over. He had been waiting in Charleston for a connection, a friend of an old friend, who had driven the first leg, down from Philadelphia. I'm taking her the rest of the way, he said. The rest of the way was to Los Angeles, where drugs and car would be handed off again and payment made.

It's a typical mule job, he told her as he drove down the coast. Pure transportation. No production, no distribution. Easiest way to make a living that I ever found. I did it once before, six, seven years ago. One run'll make you enough to live on for eight months, a year if you're careful. Which is what I am. I got used to the swamp, don't get me wrong. I respect a working man. But deals like this come along sometimes and I think that's the universe's way of saying, shake it up, man, make a change, hit the road.

The universe. She liked the thought of that. Really, she had nothing to lose.

They broke into the meth that afternoon in a hotel room in Carabelle, Florida, where she stood on the fourth-floor balcony in her underwear, listening to the tide coming in, and understood that her blood was an ocean, too, it ebbed and flowed. She smelled the salt, licked her sweaty arm to taste it.

■ ■

He talked a blue streak—the Volkswagen was blue—across the bright Gulf Coast. They were not taking the main highways. They were taking the smaller roads, the older roads, he said. They stuck close to the shoreline, drove four or five hours a day. Eli always drove and she sat back and let his voice thrum through her. It settled into her, into the hollow places—sinuses, throat, her hollow bones—and vibrated there, soothing, like the sea.

There was such joy in the world, she thought, and joy was green, like jade. Words produced their own auras, tinted atmospheres. Love was green, too, but like a lime. There was an alliterative logic to it, she realized, excitedly, somewhere in Louisiana, as they passed another smoldering refinery. Peace was purple. Glory was gold, and so was grace.

Grace, he said. Glory. Now those are words for these parts. This is real fire and brimstone country. He rolled down his window, took a deep breath. Smell the sulfur?

Then he began a long story about a man he had known once in Mississippi, a cotton farmer, whose father and grandfather were cotton farmers, who was going broke because of falling cotton prices, and who one day went to church to talk to the pastor about it. The whole time the farmer talked, the pastor was shelling and eating peanuts, and when he was done talking the pastor said something about blessed are the poor, for theirs is the kingdom of God. Then he went on eating peanuts. And so the farmer went home and decided to plant peanuts instead of cotton. The point of the story— the moral, it seemed—was that the farmer got very rich.

■■

They skirted the cities to avoid attention. Eli drove the speed limit. They gave a false name at hotels and paid with cash. They were careful, but she knew it didn't matter. The air was dense with destiny. They were in the care of the universe.

Outside of Houston, he talked about his mother. Kind, kind, very kind and gentle. A good woman of the old sort, not found anymore. Grew up poor in a logging town, in a prefab house with no foundation, where the dust just breathed up through the floor. She loved us. She did her best for us. I mourn her every day. Her and all her kind, all the old daughters of Eve who carried the sadness of our lost world. Who carries it now? No one. It's dispersed, diffuse, the very air we breathe. I see her at the kitchen sink, in that ratty robe, looking out the window. What was she looking for? What was she looking for? Her heart was always breaking. Then it broke, and she died, right there on the kitchen floor.

She was choked up, crying, remembering her own mother, standing out on the front lawn with her mouth open and her arms raised to the sky.

He was quiet. He was waiting for her to speak, to tell him why she was crying.

But she said, Talk. Keep talking.

III.

Her mother had worked as a secretary in Topeka. She was always on and off her meds. When she was on her meds she dressed every morning, fixed her hair, came home, made dinner, watched TV through flat eyes. Sometimes she seemed to fall asleep there on the couch, sitting up with her head drooped and her mouth gaping, but her eyes were open, flat. She said, it feels like my blood's turned to water. She said, it feels like my brain's got a flat tire. Grace wanted to help. She made tea. She nuzzled her mother's leg, like a dog.

When she was off her meds, she made elaborate ice cream sundaes. She took Grace to the fair in Hutchinson and spent a whole week's pay and they drove home with their faces stained with ice cream and cotton candy and two goldfish which they put in a mixing bowl and found floating there the next day. She decided to put a swimming pool in the yard and together they dug a shallow hole, filled it with water from the hose, took off their clothes, and wallowed in the mud.

It got worse as she got older. Her mother heard things on the radio, messages from God. Grace asked why she couldn't hear them, too, and her mother said, Because you're trapped in your body. You're all closed off. I'm open. Do you understand? I've opened up, so I can feel everything.

The spring that Grace was six her mother put up an eight-foot radio antennae on the front lawn and strapped herself to it with a complicated homemade harness. Grace watched through the living room window, scared, as her mother stood in the yard with her mouth open and her arms raised to the sky. Soon they came and got her in an ambulance, and then a kind white-haired woman came and watched TV with Grace until her grandparents arrived. She spent a month on the farm while her mother was in the hospital. When her mother came to get her, Grace ran to the car to hug her, and her mother hugged her back, but Grace could tell that she had changed. Her eyes were flat. She was closed off again.

They went back to Topeka and lived together for a year before her mother left again. Dropped her off at her grand-parents' farm and ran off with Roland, a tall, thin man with a sharp face and hair slicked back, who talked about God's will in a voice that crackled and spit like a downed power line. Gave her a doll and told her to be good.

IV.

They drove north toward Dallas, where they stopped in a trailer park and picked up a friend of Eli's. He was built like a heavyweight. She offered him the front seat but he shook his head, squeezed his bulk into the back where he sat with his knees up by his chin. His name was Brian and he had a bad mouth. His lips were always moving, squirming, as if they wanted to crawl off his face.

Me and Brian go way back, Eli told her. All the way back to the Northern Nevada Correctional Facility in '98. We're taking him all the way.

■■

In Dallas they checked into a suite at the Hilton. Brian had a vial of cocaine that they added to the mix, and that put an edge on the night, shook things into focus. (Things had gotten out of focus, she realized.) She was hungry. She felt like a predator, a wolf. They ordered steaks up to the room and she picked one up with her hands and bit into it, growling. She did it for them, to make them laugh. They laughed. Look at my girl, Eli said to Brian, winking. She's wild. She's a wild animal, once you get to know her.

They went out to a club that Brian knew. It was all fake leather and maroon carpet, music that was noise to her. She and Eli had sex in the bathroom and came out to find Brian in an argument with a man wearing a bolo tie. Eli walked up to him, flicked the tie with his finger. The man sighed, said, fuck this, and turned away. Triumph was maroon, like the carpet. The logic had changed.

There were other places. The night smeared. There was the purple light of dawn. When she woke up in the afternoon, she was alone and ravenous. Almost all of the food they had ordered the night before was still there on the table. They had barely touched it. She sat down and ate, looking at the wallpaper, thinking nothing. Her mind was cauterized, sealed shut.

When they came in, the men were angry and in a rush. There had been a dispute about the bill. They had to leave in a hurry. Pack your things, Eli told her. She looked at her unopened backpack and shrugged.

■ ■

Let's slow down a little, now. Let's take stock. We have a car full of drugs and no money. So what we've got is a liquidity problem. Cash flow. And that's a good problem to have. The drugs in this car are worth a million, easy. And that's wholesale. Maybe two million retail. One pound of this stuff—he reached across her lap to open the glove compartment, took out a bag to show them—is a steal at ten grand. So what we do is, change our business model. Adapt. Move into distribution.

She had only been half-listening, letting his voice flow through her like a current, but now something snapped like a static shock. What happened to transportation? she said, suddenly nervous. Why don't we just drive straight to L.A., no stops, hand off the car, get paid, and go to the beach?

Her voice sounded strange in her ears, as if it came from someone else. Afterwards she wasn't sure she had spoken at all, but the word beach lingered in her mind, white gulls swooping across that blue background.

Thing is, Eli said, these guys expect a little graft. It's built into their equation. One, two pounds go missing, and they write it off, you know?

A business expense, Brian said, his big head jutting up between the front seats.

Exactly. So we're back to liquidity, which is essentially supply and demand. We've got the supply, and we need to go where the demand is.

Where? she asked, from somewhere else. Go where?

■ ■

They drove through the night and when the red rim of the world appeared they were in Kansas. She had slept. Brian was sleeping, somehow, with his head hanging between his knees. Eli had not slept. He had snorted bumps of meth off a key.

Here we are, he said as the light bloomed around them. The broken heartland.

Flat, flat nothing. An endless road. Brown November fields.

Later that morning he pointed something out to her. It was a cliff, a long stone face rising from the prairie. It looked like one half of a low hill had fallen away and left a wall of sheer rock. It looked as if it had been carved out by the blade of a huge shovel.

A buffalo jump, he said. The Indians would put wolf skins on to scare the buffalo, make them stampede. Imagine. Like an earthquake, hundreds of them, and you in a wolf skin running and whooping, the buffalo so scared they just run off the cliff and break their legs. Imagine that.

She did imagine, closed her eyes and felt the ground shake. She felt the cliff approaching, the empty space beneath her feet, her own weight pulling her down.

After that it's just mopping up, he said. Target practice for the kids.

V.

In her dream she was a buffalo, running alongside a thousand others. They were making the earth shake. They were breathing hard with their huge heads lowered. She could not see anything except for their brown bodies and the blank sky above.

Then they fell away in front of her and then she was falling, too. And then she was not a buffalo but a bird—a long, white bird; a heron—and she was not falling but flying, and she looked behind her and all the other buffalo had turned into birds, too. The moment they went over the cliff they transformed and rose gracefully into the air. They were flying. They were following her, up.

VI.

In a town called Hugoton they left her in the Greyhound station while they went out to test the market, as Eli put it. She watched the people waiting and boarding their buses. Hunched and glassy-eyed, they lined up for a bus which eventually departed from beneath the aluminum canopy. Then another identical bus took its place, and another identical line of people. Time passed differently in a bus station, she thought. It didn't go straight along but in circles, round and round.

She'd been in too many bus stations to count, but they all circled around the first one, in Wichita, like ripples spreading in a pond. She'd been seventeen. Her mother had been gone for years and she had been living with her grandparents on the sunflower farm. One day she came home from school and was heading up the stairs to her room when her eyes caught on something blue, a postcard that lay in a small pile of letters on the low table in the hall, where her grandmother always set the mail. The postcard had a bird on it, a bluebird, and on the front it said, The Eastern Bluebird: The State Bird of New York. On the back, written in the crouching, slanted handwriting she would recognize anywhere, were her name and a few lines:

Darling. I am spread too thin. I feel like I might float away. I love you.

Her life on the farm had not been a bad one. Her grandparents were kind, loving. She liked school. She played volleyball. But as soon as the postcard flew into her life, none of that mattered anymore. For the first time, she felt the pull of destiny. She felt like an actress in a play, being given a cue from offstage. It was just a matter now of saying her line.

The next day, she sat in the bus station in Wichita, waiting for the bus to New York. In her backpack she had some clothes and a small gold bar she had stolen from the safe her grandfather kept under the stairs. He was a good man, distrustful of the banking system. He kept a safe full of ten-ounce gold bricks which he had shown her once, explaining inflation. Her grandmother had sat with her at the kitchen table every day, helping her with her homework.

Now, in Hugoton, she tried to remember her grandmother's voice. She tried to remember the golden sunflower fields in summer, so bright it was as if they were from another time, a prehistoric gold, the yellow blood of the earth. She closed her eyes and tried to raise that color in her mind, but could only touch the edge of it.

She could leave now, she knew. She could just get on a bus. They wouldn't find her. They probably wouldn't even look. She could get on a bus to Wichita, go back to the farm. It had only been five years since she left. Her grandparents would still be there. They would take her in.

But she had abandoned them, and she was ashamed. How could she explain it all to them? To her grandmother with her soft voice and knotted, arthritic hands? No. It was easier to succumb, to yield to destiny, let herself be carried by it, float.

VII.

They came back to the bus station at one o'clock. Eli gave her a sandwich. He had a little money and he was happy, strutting. He said, this place is going to suit us just fine.

Someone had told them about a place nearby, an abandoned town where they could squat for a while. They found it twenty minutes down a nameless highway, past a sign that said Woods, Kansas (Unincorporated). It was not a town. It was three houses, an old grain elevator, and a barn, all in various states of disrepair, nestled in a copse of trees—maples, cedars, Russian olives—crouched in an expanse of bare winter fields.

Just here for the taking, Eli said. A whole town. Fruit off the vine.

In one of the houses they found an iron woodstove in the kitchen and two springbox beds with mattresses. There were a few old pots and pans and plates, dusty. Eli found a dull axe in the barn and used it to rip planks off the barn walls for firewood. Brian found a pile of bricks and a piece of plywood and built a table in the kitchen. She got into the spirit, too, swept the floors with the branch of a spruce tree. They brought the two beds into the kitchen for warmth and lit a fire in the stove. The room grew warm. With the money they'd made that afternoon, they'd bought bread and cheese and eggs and bologna. She fried the pink meat on the stove for them, as her mother had done for her. The men watched her cook. She felt them watching, hungry.

I'm not much for religion, Eli said when the food was ready, but I am humble. I understand my own insignificance. I can acknowledge it. And I'd be the last one to deny that there are miracles in this world. And this feels like a miracle. And I think we ought to pause and recognize that. Say grace. We are grateful. For this place. For this bounty. For each other. The universe provideth.

Amen.

■■

They settled into a routine. It was domestic. In the morning, she cooked breakfast and the men went off to work—selling drugs in Hugoton—and then she had the day to herself. The first few days, she got high and set to work on the house, cleaning and trying to add small pieces of charm. They brought her a sponge and soap and she scrubbed the floors. At the edge of a field there was a well pump that still worked, though she knew it would soon freeze. In one of the other houses she found yellow plaid curtains, which she took and hung. She found a checkered sheet and spread it over the table to hide the ugly wood.

In the late afternoons, the men came back and she made dinner. If they had made any money, they brought groceries or small things for the house: candles, an oil lamp, sheets and blankets from the Salvation Army. Eli got her a new coat. It was for a man and much too big—she could almost disappear inside it—but it was warm and she was grateful.

She could only do so much around the house, so she started taking walks through the empty fields. Alone in the middle of that nothing she sometimes had a wonderful feeling, a kind of communion with the fields and air. She felt porous, permeable. In the trees around the town there were often crows, hundreds of them squawking, and she fantasized that they were her, or she was them, the whole group of them, ready to rise—dissolve, disperse, disappear—into the big slate sky.

VIII.

Increasingly, the men came back sullen, irritable.

We've exhausted the demand here, Eli said one evening. He was in the clawfoot bathtub, which they had unscrewed from the plumbing and brought into the kitchen. (They heated water on the stove. Like pioneers, Eli had said, like bona fide hayseed homesteaders.) The kitchen was bathed in a pooling, waxy light from the candles.

Maybe we should think about moving on, Brian said from his seat at the table.

This is a good thing we've got here, Eli said. We're just not reaching a wide-enough market.

That's what I mean, Brian said. We've exhausted the market. That's what you just said.

A short pause. Then, Don't you ever tell me what I just motherfucking said.

His voice was a blade. She heard it in her teeth. She was tending the stove fire, waiting for another pot of bathwater to heat up, and she did not dare turn around to face them. The threat of violence was like the threat of snow, now, growing heavier with each passing day.

Okay, okay, Brian said. But maybe we should finish the mule. We could make L.A. in two long days, I bet.

And leave all this behind?

In his voice now there was a joke, and so she turned away from the stove to face them, eager to ride the downslope of tension. Eli was smiling and gesturing towards her from the tub.

She can come, too, Brian said. And then, to her: Don't you want to go to the beach, sweetheart?

In a flash of smooth, liquid motion, Eli rose from the tub and stepped across the kitchen to Brian, and before she let out her breath he had somehow acquired a kitchen knife and was holding the tip of it to Brian's throat.

Don't fucking talk to her, he said. Do you understand? Don't even look at her.

All the air had gone out of the room. She gasped and brought her hand to her mouth. Neither man said anything for a moment. Eli stood dripping on the floor, steam rising from his skin, his flaccid penis hanging off his body like a pale leech. Brian was staring up at him with cold, narrow eyes.

Finally, Eli lowered the knife and backed off a few steps. Brian rose slowly to his feet and put on his coat.

Where do you think you're going? Eli said.

For a walk, Brian said. He turned and went out the door and, for a few moments, they were left in silence. Then they heard the sound of the Volkswagen start outside and Eli ran out after him, shouting, Hey! Hey! She stayed where she was, listening to the receding sound of the car engine as it pulled away. Waiting for what would happen next. She could feel the cold air coming through the open door. On the stove, the water began to boil.

Eli came back inside and closed the door behind him. He'll be back, he said. Mark my words. He'll be back before morning.

What if he doesn't come back? she said. Most of the drugs were still in the car.

He'll be back, Eli said again. He picked up the pipe from the counter and took a long hit, and then he stepped slowly back into the bath. Let's freshen her up, he said, pointing to the pot of water on the stove. She lifted it and poured it into the tub near his feet. He sighed with pleasure, leaned his head back, and closed his eyes.

They waited, smoked. Eli talked and talked. The Interstate Highway System. West African religion. Italian anarchism. The aching desire to know God. She settled into bed, listening. She rode his voice all the way through the night.

As dawn approached, Eli became more and more anxious. Where is this motherfucker? he said, pacing back and forth across the kitchen. I knew it was a bad idea to bring him into this.

Near daybreak, they heard a car pull up. Eli was sitting at the table, talking, but when they heard the car he went silent.

For a moment she imagined that, instead of Brian, it was the police arriving, come to take them off to prison. Or the ambulance, come to take her away. She imagined the same paramedic who'd taken her mother years before: that boy-faced, crew-cutted man who'd cut the straps of the harness she'd used to tie herself to the radio antennae. Or maybe it was her grandfather in his run-down red pickup. Maybe he had been looking for her all this time, driving around Kansas with her picture, stopping at every truck stop and motel. Maybe he would take her home.

The door opened and Brian came in and shut it behind him.

So, Eli said. His hands were clasped in front of him. He had the bearing of an exasperated parent. Do you want to tell us where the fuck you've been all night?

Without speaking, Brian took something from his coat pocket and set it down on the table. She couldn't see what it was from where she lay on the bed. Eli frowned. Then he reached across the table and picked it up and she could see that it was a gun. He held it up to the pale light that came in through the windows, examining it.

Well, he said after a moment, one eyebrow raised. Well, well.

■■

For two days she listened to them plotting, scheming. They would rob a bank. No, an armored car. A liquor store. A gas station. She would drive the getaway car. No, she would provide a diversion, pretend to be a bystander. They smoked, drew maps. When they got tired, they shot the gun off in the fields. She watched them, swaddled in her coat. The sky was low and leaden. The noise from the gun swelled out into that space and she felt the sounds reverberate through her. She rippled like the air.

I've been on both ends of a pointed gun, Eli said, back in the kitchen, and let me assure you that there are no two feelings more different. The problem comes if you confuse the two. I've seen it happen. I've seen a man with a gun in his face grow bold, fearless. Lucky for him the gun wasn't loaded. I've often wondered, did he know? Did he sense it somehow? On the other hand, I've seen a man with a gun get cold feet and start crying. Pointing a gun at a guy and just blubbering. Can you imagine that?

What about the drugs? she said, suddenly lucid. What about the plan?

Every so often, she had a moment like this, when a window opened in her mind and she saw the situation, briefly, from the outside. What were they doing here? What happened to California? It was as if the arrival of the gun had erased all previous motion and set them on an entirely new course. In retrospect, their whole excursion looked suddenly like a series of accidents, completely divorced from any plan or providence. Anxiety fizzed up behind her eyes.

It's called adaptation, baby, Eli said. The introduction of a new element demands a recalibration of the formula. Now we have a new variable to figure for.

She could not remember the last time she'd slept. Eli offered her the pipe, but she shook her head. Her face was suddenly wet. She was crying big silent tears.

Oh sweetheart, Eli said. His voice sounded genuinely sad. You're carrying too much. Your load has become too heavy.

I know just the thing, Brian said. He got up and went out to the car, and when he came back inside a minute later, he was holding the brick of heroin, smiling.

■ ■

She lay on the bed in the kitchen and found she could go anywhere in her mind, touch any feeling. She thought of her mother strapped to the radio antennae and cried, thinking how easy it was, after all, to tap into everything. All it required was to become nothing, dissolve the borders of yourself and let the world in.

She went to her grandparents' house in Wichita. She floated through every room, saw everything in perfect detail, the pictures on the wall, the stain on the wallpaper in the dining room, the deer's head mounted above her grandfather's writing desk, the beaded chain that hung from the light over the kitchen table, the steel safe in the closet under the stairs, where her grandfather kept the gold bricks. When he had shown her, she sat on his lap at his desk chair and the light had gleamed off the gold and she had touched it, very smooth, and outside in the summer air there were the sunflowers rustling, glorious, and she filled her mind with that gold color and she felt that happiness was flowing out of her, out of her fingers, out of her mouth.

When she opened her eyes Eli and Brian were both watching her intently. They, too, were bathed in gold.

Honey, Eli said. Sweetheart, can you tell me where this farm is?

She laughed. Of course she could.

Eli smiled, too, and took her hand. The universe provideth, he said.

IX.

When she woke up, she was alone. Pale light came in through the window above the sink. She sat up in bed, blinking, feeling herself come in and out of focus. Her head hurt and her mouth was very dry.

She stood and went to the sink, looked out the window at the fields. She frowned, trying to think. What had she done? What had she told them? Were they on their way to Wichita now, Brian in the front seat, the gun in the glove compartment? She imagined her grandfather looking down the barrel of the gun, scared. Yes, terrified. But also sad, disappointed.

■ ■

She left the kitchen and went up into the barn. She took the blankets and climbed into the hayloft and made herself a nest. Eli had left her a few grams of heroin and a brick of meth, more than she could ever use (perhaps as payment, she thought absently). If she put enough of it into her body, she would dissolve the borders of herself completely. She had everything she needed.

She did not feel afraid. It was pleasant in the barn, soft. As a girl she had spent hours by herself in the hayloft of her grandfather's barn, making straw dolls, composing songs, reading. Below her the sunflower fields rolled out like a golden quilt.

From her nest, she could see through the big door in the hayloft across the fields to some trees and, as the light faded, she could see the red lights on top of the radio towers in the distance, blinking.

X.

She'd arrived in New York with no idea where to go. She'd sat on the bench in Penn Station until they told her to leave. She'd walked the streets of Manhattan all night. Seventeen years old. In the morning she found a shop in the Village with a sign in the dirty window that said, We Buy Gold. She went in and sold the brick for three thousand dollars, more money than she could have imagined. She walked up to Central Park and checked into the first nice-looking hotel she could find. The room was incredible. She ordered room service. She sat on the bed and looked at the postcard again. She had fingered it so often that the edges were brown and thin.

Darling. I am spread too thin. I feel I might float away. I love you.

There was a postmark that said Queens, New York, but no return address.

She wandered the city in the daytime. She wanted to find her mother, but she didn't know how to look for her. She walked through Central Park. She wandered the Village. She went down to the Battery and looked out at the ocean, the Statue of Liberty, the Brooklyn Bridge, the gulls swooping over the water.

Her money went fast. She moved to a cheaper hotel. She ate two meals a day, usually in diners. She liked the city, she found. She liked being among all those people, all the stray lives she passed in the day, all the anonymous faces. She read the postcard over and over. She'd begun to feel very thin herself.

One day, walking in Chinatown, she passed the police station. On a whim, she went inside and told them she was looking for her mother, gave them her mother's name. She waited for an hour, until an officer called her over to his desk and told her that her mother had killed herself a month before. Jumped from the top of a building in Queens.

His voice went inside of her and coiled up there, dense and heavy, as if she had swallowed a stone.

The officer gave her an address and she went there on the subway. The neighborhood was quiet and run-down, grey brick buildings, gutters choked with trash. The door to the building was unlocked and she went up a dank stair-well to the third floor. She knocked on the door of the apartment, but no one answered. She knocked again and waited, then tried the doorknob and found it open.

She was hit with a rancid smell, vomit and charred metal. She covered her mouth and nose and tried not to retch. The room was very dim and it took a moment before she could make out her surroundings. All the windows had been covered with cardboard. She saw a couch and a coffee table. She felt strangely calm; it didn't occur to her to be afraid. She waded through a layer of trash to the hallway and checked each room: two bedrooms, each with a stained, bare mattress on the floor. The whole apartment gave off an air of abandonment.

On the floor in the second bedroom she found two hypodermic needles and another postcard, this one with a picture of the Empire State Building on the front. It was blank. Had her mother wanted to write to her again? Perhaps, she thought, her mother had bought them both because she hadn't been able to choose one. Perhaps she had looked at them for a long time, trying to decide which postcard Grace would like best.

She left the apartment, started back down the stairs. Then she stopped, turned around and went up instead, to the roof. The building was five stories high. The sky was grey. She could see the rooftops of lower buildings, brown water towers, in the middle-distance a busy highway. She walked to the edge and looked down at the sidewalk below. She felt heavy, weighted down. She felt how quickly she would fall, how hard she would hit the ground.

After a few moments, she went back down the stairs. That night, she went to the Port Authority to catch a bus back to Kansas. She bought a ticket but when it came time to board she stayed where she was, seated on a cold bench. She watched her bus leave. She was thinking of her grandparents, who would be out of their minds with worry. She hadn't even left a note. They would have no idea where to look for her. They would blame themselves, wonder what they had done, how they had driven her off. If she came back, they would cry and clutch her. All would be forgiven. There was another bus an hour later.

But she couldn't bring herself to get on that one, either. She remembered when her mother had gotten out of the hospital years before, when she'd come to pick her up at her grandparents'. Her mother had hugged her and told her how much she'd missed her. But even then, Grace had known that it wasn't really her mother, that her mother was still somewhere else. That she hadn't come back at all.

Near midnight she was approached by a thin, lanky boy with pockmarks on his face and scabs on his knuckles. Hey, he said. Are you hungry? She nodded, and he produced half of a sandwich from the pocket of his coat. She looked at him. His eyes were deep-set and bleary, but kind. He smiled, showing a single gold tooth.

She would never get on a bus, she knew. She would never go back.

She took the sandwich, wolfed it down in seconds.

XI.

End at the end, at the beginning of a cold grey day, in the barn, up in the hayloft, alone. In Woods, Kansas, waking in her nest of blankets and looking out through the open hayloft door across the bare December fields. She rises, wraps a blanket around her shoulders and walks to the edge of the hayloft door. She is perhaps thirty feet off the ground and from that height she can see across the fields, across the blank colorless world, to a distant stand of trees. She watches as a cloud of crows surges from the trees, swoops and circles in the air. She remembers her dream, and she imagines flying out across the fields to meet them. She can still touch that feeling of weightlessness, flight.

■ ■

A figure emerges from the trees, walking across the fields toward the barn. She watches, not trusting her vision. Minutes pass. The figure approaches, takes shape. A tan uniform and hat. A cop. A woman. Approaching the barn but looking straight-ahead, not up.

Hello? she called from below. Is anyone here?

When it was time for supper grandmother would yell up to the hayloft, where she was hiding. Sometimes, she would wait to answer, wondering what would happen if she didn't, if she might be invisible.

She does not speak. The woman walks below her, stops. And then, finally, she looks up.

Holy! she says, startled. She takes a step back and brings her hand to her chest. She is young, in her twenties. She has straight brown hair cut to her shoulders. Her shoulders are slight, but she stands sturdily, looks strong. She lets out a breath and says, Geez, you scared me. What the hell are you doing up there?

Still, she does not answer. She feels so airy, so insubstantial, that she does not trust herself to make a sound. She looks back toward the trees, where the crows have settled again.

Hey, the woman says below. Hey! Listen, I got a report that there were some men living out here, some gunshots?

Do you know anything about that? Are you here alone? Are you hurt? I can help you. Are you okay?

Her voice is kind and warm. She feels it loosening something in her, thawing out the ocean of her blood. She is cold. She is shaking. Something about that voice, the gentleness of it. A woman's voice seeping slowly into her and all of a sudden she does not want to dissolve. She wants something else.

Who are you? the woman asks. What's your name?

She wants to hone the edges of herself. She wants a new crisp version of herself to emerge, be born, from the blurry background of her life. Deliverance.

Grace, she says.

And then again, because she stuttered: My name is Grace.

Prairie Fire, 1899

First there was nothing, just the silent, empty prairie and the darkness lying heavy over it.

Then there was the train, the great black engine that had steamed out of Fargo and hurled itself west across the plains, making speed because its cars were empty of freight and because every hour the engineer yelled back to the stoker to keep the fire roaring. Boiling, furious, the train heaved through the night and through the liquid pre-dawn glow and as the sun floated up over the eastern rim of the world the train was still churning west and towing that blazing globe behind it, pulling it up out of the dark. Midmorning, the train stopped in the coal town of Sims, North Dakota, where it took on four cars of brown lignite and then went on, aimed at Tacoma. Ten miles outside of Sims, the stoker cleared the ash pan, tossed the white-hot clinker out of the engine into the vacant prairie, where the wheatgrass and bluestem were October-brown and bending in a western breeze.

That breeze blew back to Sims, where it was Sunday, Sabbath, and so after the hopper cars had been loaded the workweek was over and the forty-three men employed by the Northern Pacific Coal Company lined up to get their pay. Colonel Bly—the mine manager—sat at the table he set up every week on the platform at the depot, smoking his cigar and scrawling his signature across the bottom of the company scrip. At his right elbow stood his foreman—a tall, glowering Swede, name of Knutson—who looked up each miner's name in his ledger as they approached and saw there what weight of coal had been logged for the week and calculated the man's pay in his head to tell Colonel Bly, who wrote it out on the scrip and signed. After that weekly sacrament the men were free until first shift started the next morning. Some attended services at one of the three churches in town—Catholic, Lutheran, Presbyterian—which were postponed every Sunday until after the train had been loaded. Others, homesteaders, went to buy provisions for the week at the general store before starting the long walk out to their sod houses and farms. The rest made their way to the saloons, where they would spend a good part of their wages and where, later, some commotion—insults, challenges, bets, fistfights— could be expected.

But before all that, during those short, bright hours after being paid, their time was their own and they were free to do as they pleased. And those were the sweetest hours of the week. Because these were men who had been underground, breathing the black dust, crawling on their knees through the cold catacombs they had blown open with dynamite, checking the flames of their lamps to make sure that they did not burn green from the poison gas that was the earth's dank breath. And now, aboveground, they could breathe the free air in daylight and smell the soft breeze that came from the west.

By noon that breeze already carried the smell of smoke, though faintly, feebly. Norma Goodwin caught a hint of it as she crossed Main Street to visit her friend Joanne Crocker, who was sick with fever. She paused and lifted her nose to the west, but she couldn't locate the smell. It was stronger an hour later, when the congregation of the Sims Evangelical Lutheran Church trickled into the street. They smelled it, but no warning was raised: it could have been anything, a trash fire, just the usual output of a dozen stoves all warming Sunday dinner. Irvin Olin, who worked for the railroad overseeing the depot, was playing cards with August Weinrich, Sr. when they caught the smell in the air. They were sitting on the porch of the depot out on the edge of town and when he smelled it Olin stood up and breathed and looked off to the west from beneath the brim of his hat, but he didn't see anything, just sky and prairie, both yawning empty.

The first to see the smoke was old William Crump, known locally as Uncle Willy. In the war he had fought under General Sherman, at Shiloh, at Vicksburg, at Chattanooga, Atlanta, Savannah, Columbia, and afterwards he had come west to Dakota Territory and worked for the railroad before his homestead section came through: one hundred acres of flat grassland where Crump tried to live and raise grain for five years. But out there alone on the lonely prairie his mind had turned back to the war and he had begun to live simultaneously in both times: while running a team across his field he was riding slowly through the Georgia swamp; while shooting antelope he was aiming at a Confederate position entrenched in the rocks along a stream. At all times he carried in his belt a pistol he had recovered from a dead Confederate officer in 1865. He had taken a ball in the right shoulder at Vicksburg, and he could still feel it in the mornings, stiff, aching, and throughout his day he brought his left hand unthinkingly to that place. When it became too much for him, out there alone, he had moved back to town. On Sundays he bought a bottle of whiskey and drank it on the roof of the grain elevator, the highest place in town, where he could see for miles and project his memory out into that blank open space and overlook the past from the safe high ground. To the passerby in the street below he seemed a lonely watchman, scanning the western plains, waiting for something to come up over the horizon. But that afternoon, when something finally did, he did not sound any alarm. He took a drink from his bottle and raised his left hand to his shoulder, to the scar that was there beneath his shirt.

Nearly an hour later, Thorsten Larsen burst into the Mineshaft Saloon, yelling, Fire! Fire! Larsen homesteaded a plot three miles outside of town and was generally considered odd: at harvest-time each year he refused to help with the threshing on the grounds that the work would stiffen his fingers, which he wanted to keep limber for his Hardanger fiddle. He had brought the violin with him from Norway in 1891 and often talked about it and displayed it to visitors, but no one had ever heard him play it. It was now packed along with the other things Larsen had managed to salvage in his cart just outside the saloon, where his wife, Laura, sat holding a rescued shoat in her arms. Small mind was paid to Larsen at first. He was yelling, Fire! Fire!

and speaking rapid Norwegian, but consumed as they were in their other pursuits the miners did not register what he said for some minutes, until like a wave the news spread through the barroom and then in a great rush the men hurried through the door to see for themselves.

There it was, now: the low grey smear along the western horizon.

For a moment the men looked out in silence, stunned. Then their shock thawed into panic. Three men were sent into town to raise the alarm. The others—about a dozen in total—ran to the general store, where they told Sam Fletcher what was happening: a mile out, maybe; wind's blowing straight in; be here in a few hours. There were several shovels in the store and they took them out past the depot and began digging a trench there, carving up the dry grass around the town.

Just as they began to dig, the bells from the Lutheran Church rang out—one of the messengers had thought of that—and the sound was so incongruous at that quiet time of the Sabbath as to call people from their homes. Soon a small crowd had gathered in the middle of the main street. As the news circulated, their voices grew louder and more frantic: Should we leave? Sure it's coming this way? What about the children?

Rosa Anderson stepped up onto the porch of the post office and raised her voice above the others. Rosa was married to George Anderson, the baker, but before that she had been an opera singer in Chicago. She had stood on stage at Crosby's Opera House and thrown her voice into the teeming crowd: Rossini, Bellini, Donizetti, Verdi. She had been a rising star, billed the Belle Canto of Chicago, until the great fire razed Crosby's and most of downtown. Rosa had planned to go east after that, but in the spring she had come down with a bad bout of pneumonia which collapsed part of her lung and ruined her career for good, and when she was finally able to leave her bed, she married the sad, sweet man who had visited her every day in the hospital and filled her ears with his dreams of going west: sad, sweet George Anderson. Now, nearly thirty years later, Rosa filled her deep lungs with air and bellowed from the porch: All right! All right! Now, friends, what we have here is an emergency. We're going to need to act quickly. No time to waste. We've all helped to build this town and now we're all going to have to help save it.

Under Rosa's direction it was decided that the children should be taken to the only building in town that was not made of wood: the new brick schoolhouse, just completed that summer. Simon Lewis, who operated the telegraph, ran to the depot to send messages to all neighboring towns and request help from the village of Glen Ullin, which had a fire department. The town-women dispersed to see to their children and their homes; their husbands were dispatched to the edge of town to help the others dig.

Out there, at the trench, the scrape and churn of the shovels had fallen into a steady rhythm. The sound of the digging floated up to a sparsely-furnished bedroom on the second floor of the Mineshaft Saloon, where Fannie Hall sat brushing her hair in front of her dressing mirror. When she heard it, Hall rose and went to the room's small window and opened it and stuck her head out and saw the men digging there below and called out, Hey! What're you all doing digging in the dirt down there? My girls are trying to sleep!

It's a prairie fire! Jay Knowles shouted back. Better get your girls waked up!

Fire! Hall said. Well damn.

She shut the window and sat down heavily at the dressing table. Hall was the madam of the small bordello that operated above the bar. Before coming to Sims she had worked in a brothel in Minot, where she had met and married a man named Joseph Blackburn, who had staked a mining claim three miles south of Sims and died a year later when the entrance to the shaft collapsed, burying him alive. That same spring, Hall changed her name and opened her own house of ill fame, and now was one of Sims's wealthiest citizens. After thinking for a few moments, she took a long pull on her cigarette and then rose again and went out of the room and walked down the hallway, banging on each of the doors and shouting, Wake up! Wake up!

One by one the three sleepy-eyed women opened their doors and peeked their heads out into the hallway. What is it, Fannie? It's just three o'clock.

It's a damn fire! Hall yelled. You all hurry up and get yourselves dressed and ready to get to work!

Half an hour later the four women had dressed and tied their hair back and joined the men at the trench, where they dug with whatever tools were at hand—picks and a rusty ax—and by then other men worked alongside with scythes, cutting down the tall grass and raking it away. Two plows were hitched and their iron blades carved beneath the sod and turned it over, leaving a ragged scar in the prairie.

Great flocks of birds were flying overhead and soon the animals began to appear—antelope, deer, rabbits, coyotes, running alone or in pairs; and even some fugitive farm animals: horses, pigs, a few sheep—all fleeing, panting, tongues lolling out of their mouths. More homesteaders were riding into town with their carts packed high, and like grim harbingers they delivered the news: it was moving fast, due east; a mile west of town the very sky was made of smoke. Some of the farmers stopped to help, but others, less hopeful, drove on, headed for Sims Creek on the eastern side of town.

By four o'clock the sky had dimmed and the setting sun was veiled by smoke, a pale disc gleaming through the grey curtain. Still, looking west over the low swell of the land, the men saw nothing, just the ceaseless sway of grass. From his perch on top of the grain elevator, Uncle Willy watched and waited, and when he saw the horizon light up like a second sun was rising in the west, his old carved-from-a-mountain face cracked into a crooked smirk.

A quarter of an hour later, E.J. Burke drove his wagon into town, yelling out for a doctor. Charley Mato was pulled from the line of diggers and hurried to the wagon. Lying in the wagonbed was Burke's daughter, Stella, a girl of twelve. She was still alive, he saw; her chest rose and fell. But half her face was black, charred, the skin peeling away from her skull. Her eyes looked up blankly at nothing. Doctor Mato was a Mandan Indian and he had been educated at Carlisle before coming back to North Dakota to work for the mine. In that work he had seen men blown apart with dynamite, treated miners whose legs had been crushed in a tunnel collapse, watched men cough up dark, powdery blood. He understood that there was damage that could not be undone, things so broken they could not be fixed. Doctor Mato forced himself to meet Burke's eye and then he shook his head silently. The girl, he knew, was beyond hearing, but he could not bring himself to say any words. Likewise silent, Burke looked back, slack-jawed and red-eyed, and after a moment he lifted his hands, loose at the wrist, and Doctor Mato saw that they were also badly burned. Burke said, she went back into the barn for her calf. It was all afire but she went back in, and when she come out she was all afire, too. I put her out myself. I put her out with my hands. Seeing those hands Doctor Mato could foresee the pain that Burke would soon be in. He looked back at the girl in the wagon. She was dead. Still wordless he took Burke's elbow and led him into town, to the clinic, where he put salve on his hands and wrapped them in bandages. They left the girl in the wagon, where she lay like some terrible portent in the street, her sightless eyes still open, looking up at the sky, which was slowly dimming.

Colonel Bly, the mine manager, was looking at that same sky, standing on the porch of his house and rubbing his eyes. A moment before, he had woken from his afternoon rest to the smell of the smoke and now he looked out blinking, waiting for comprehension to jolt him fully out of sleep. His house was a half mile outside of town, near the mine, and looking west past the drab, grey mine buildings—the office and warehouse squatting in the foreground and the

hoist house and tipple towering thirty feet high above—
he could see the new red glow along the skyline. He saw
that flushed undersky and felt his guts go liquid and he
bolted off the porch and ran towards town. He was a
large bewhiskered man with a huge belly and gout in his
feet and by the time he reached the line of diggers he was
winded and could not take a breath to speak. The miners,
so accustomed to taking his orders, stopped digging for
a moment and waited for him to say something, but he
stood crouched and panting for so long that they resumed
their work. When he finally regained his breath, the colonel bellowed: The mine! You damn idiots! The mine! You
have to save the mine!

The men stopped digging again and looked out to the
northwest where the mine buildings stood in dark silhou-
ette against the purpling sky. They looked up at the mine
like their ancestors—serfs scratching in the dirt—might
have looked upon the lord's manor at dusk, with a mixture
of awe and fear and nerve-taut hatred. The colonel's exhor-
tation hung in the air until Lawrence Wilkes, a young
miner from Chicago, said: It's too late, Colonel. We got to
do our best to save the town.

There's no town without the mine, you son of a
bitch! The town *is* the mine! Jesus! Where's Knutson?
Where is he?

The men looked around but the Swede was not among
them. The colonel swore and turned and set off running
again, this time towards the mine, and the men stood for a
moment watching his lonely figure recede. Then they went
back to work.

When he reached the mine Colonel Bly thought his lungs might burst. He tore into the office and found it already in disarray. The door hung open and inside papers were scattered around the wood floor. The steel safe was gone from its place in the corner, and with it five thousand dollars' worth of twenty-dollar bills issued by the First National Bank in Williston. The Northern Pacific Coal Company was owned by the colonel's cousin, Terrence Bly, who had secured his position for him in exchange for a large investment of capital funds. Gone.

Winded, sapped of strength, the colonel sat down heavily in his chair. Knutson, he thought. It must have been the Swede. From his desk drawer he pulled two bottles: one of laudanum, which he took for his gout, and one of Kentucky Bourbon. He took a long drink of the first and followed it with a long drink of the second. Then he turned towards the small, grimy window, through which he generally surveyed the comings and goings at the mine, but through which he now watched the approaching line of fire as it swelled red against the gathering dark.

At that moment Knutson was already four miles away, riding through that dusk in the stolen wagon with the stolen safe, and by daybreak he would be in Mandan and by the next night Bismarck and then gone, swallowed up by the teeming country, Minneapolis, Chicago, St. Louis, New Orleans. Or perhaps east, Boston, New York, Philadelphia, Baltimore, or west, Denver, Seattle, San Francisco. Swallowed up. Gone.

And so in Sims, as the light leaked out of the day and the fire loomed, the residents dug their trench wider, and

others emptied their houses into carts, heaped their valu-
ables there in preparation for flight, and the children huddled in the brick schoolhouse where their teacher, Miss
Evelyn Crawford, led them through every song she knew,
and then again, the children's fearful faces looking up at
her in the light of the lantern, singing, my country 'tis of
thee, sweet land of liberty, of thee I sing. Long may our
land be bright, with freedom's holy light; protect us by thy
might, great God, our king.

Soon the fire was close enough to hear, roaring and
whooshing and spitting, gnashing its teeth. The flames
like forked tongues rose high as two men and the smoke
billowed into town and down the throats of the residents,
acrid, scorching. The diggers tied handkerchiefs across
their faces and went on working.

At six-thirty the mine caught fire. The blaze shot up
the tipple like an eruption, the wood of that tower coated
with flammable coal dust, and the flame rose thirty feet
above the prairie and waved and swayed there like a giant
red flag. Anyone in town with a sightline stopped to watch.
Soon they heard the small explosive sounds that were the
other buildings catching fire, the windows breaking from
the heat.

All eyes that watched that terrible blaze had seen others before it, and those antecessors hung before their vision
like conflagrant ghosts. Many of the trenchline men had
worked in the city factories, where the giant steel forges
were like red mouths gaping, insatiable in their hunger for
the coal that the filthy, sweating men shoveled into them
without end. Irving Olin had spent time working oil rigs in

Pennsylvania, where he had seen a fresh gush of oil ignite from a lamp and spout into the air like blood from the earth's black veins. The pastor of the Presbyterian Church was reminded of a picture he showed the children in cat-echism: four huge horsemen riding across the plains and revealing God's awful wrath in their fiery wake. Uncle Willy, still watching from his post on the grain elevator, saw in the burning mine the spirit of Columbia, where he had danced drunk in the street with the other soldiers while the city consumed itself around them. As the tipple began to collapse in a shower of sparks and flaming wood, he rose unsteadily to his feet, pulled the Confederate revolver from his belt, and fired six shots aimlessly into the blazing night.

During the great fire of Chicago, Rosa Anderson had fled through the swarming streets, the air choked by cin-ders and smoke and ashes falling around them like snow. Down Dearborn Street to the edge of Lake Michigan where thousands were waiting, surrounded by what they could save, and some of them swimming out in the freez-ing lake to get as far away from the fire as they could. She had sat on her trunk on the beach and watched the fire for hours through her scorched eyes, watched it come right up to the beach and stop there, menacing. Anderson saw the mine collapse and like a commanding general raised her voice again to the crowd assembled at the edge of town: The creek! The creek! Fall back to the creek!

Except for a few men who stayed behind to work, they left the town then. They collected their children from the schoolhouse, and carrying their things and pulling their carts and riding in their wagons with their animals in tow like a line of penitents or a troupe of circus performers they made their way east through the prairie to Sims Creek and in a slow file crossed the narrow wooden railroad bridge to the far bank, where others had already gathered. From that vantage they watched the fire approach and waited to see if the trench would hold.

And for a time it seemed that it would. The few men who stayed behind backed away from the blaze, the heat intolerable, the great wall of fire hovering at the border, coming right up to the line they had dug, looming, but not proceeding. Halted, the high flames bent forward in the wind like reaching arms. The trench was wide and curved around the whole western part of town and when he saw that the fire was stopped E. J. Macally clapped the shoulder of Jay Knowles in celebration, said, Hooo-ahh, we god-damn did it!

Then the jackrabbits appeared, running out of the blaze, disturbed from their tunnels beneath the prairie and risen to escape but too late, so that they ignited as they fled and became small fireballs barreling across the trench and into the dry grass on the other side.

When they realized what was happening, the men began swinging their shovels like mallets, stopping the flaming rodents and stomping them out. But there were dozens, hundreds. The rabbits stampeded out of the fire like a plague and the men could not keep up and small fires began burning on the town-side of the trench and soon the porch of the depot caught fire. The men rushed to put it out, filled tubs of water from the pump there and threw them at the burning porch, but the fire was too hot and they could not get close enough. Jay Knowles said, I'll get closer and you all throw water on me so I don't catch fire, too. They fought the fire that way for a quarter of an hour, but soon it reached the roof of the porch and caught the shingles there and the ashes and cinders blew in the wind and landed in the livery, in the dry hay of the stables. And that hay started the building burning and the cinders from that fire began to fly, as well, and the rabbits kept coming as if from some endless supply and the men were so tired they could barely walk, and finally they fell back, stumbled down to the creek, where along with the others they watched the town begin to burn.

They were all there, watching. Norma Goodwin and Irvin Olin and August Weinrich, Jr. and Thorsten Larsen and his wife, Laura, and Sam Fletcher and Fannie Hall and Doctor Mato and Lawrence Wilkes and Jay Knowles and Evelyn Crawford and E.J. Burke and E.J. Macally and Simon Lewis and Rosa Anderson and sad, sweet George Anderson, who was weeping quietly into his handkerchief, and all the residents of Sims and of the homesteads that stretched for ten miles across the prairie, one hundred and thirty people gathered in the dark along the river.

Not all, though. Not the Burkes' daughter Stella, dead. Not Knutson the Swede, escaped. Not Colonel Bly, dead. Not Uncle Willy Crump, who had fallen from the water tower and lay broken and cruciform in the street. Not Joanne Crocker, forgotten, sick with fever, very soon to burn alive in the bedroom of her house.

From that safe distance the rest of them watched their town burn and they breathed a silent clegy.

They had all had dreams and those dreams had driven them west, to America, Dakota, Sims. They had ridden that black train, led by their belief that beyond the western horizon their bright dream lay crouched and waiting.

But those dreams had been heavy, too, and they had carried them while they worked, while they sweated in the factories and busted sod and lay on their backs in the mine while their lungs blackened, paid a pittance in company scrip while their children were hungry and sick. They had slept with the dreams perched on their chests in their dirty bunks and miserable sod houses. They had seen violence done in service of those dreams and many had done violence themselves.

Let us watch them, now, as they stand on the riverbank, watching the fire. Let us watch them watching and imagine their dreams burning off like fog. Let us imagine that at that moment they abandoned their ideas of progress, of destiny. That they took the train back east and stayed.

And let us imagine that a strange exuberance spread among them, tired as they were, and as they watched the buildings catch fire, one by one, their exuberance grew into a kind of joy. They were wretched. They were poor. They understood that at any time a fire could raze their dreams to nothing, or if not a fire then a drought or plague or tornado or quake or flood would wash away whatever paltry progress they had made, and that each such cataclysm was trivial, just a sneer across the earth's ageless face, and that in the face of that fire and all other fires and all other forces of the world they were but nothing. And in that knowledge let us imagine that they felt relief, and joy, and fellowship.

E.J. Macally turned to Jay Knowles and smiled slightly and said, Rabbits. Well I'll be damned. I never thought of those damn rabbits.

Then he began to laugh, and Knowles joined him, and others, and soon there were many laughing together. In the morning they would wake and sift through the burned wreckage of their lives and face their blank, uncertain futures, but now they were laughing and touching each other's arms and hands and washing each others' soot-blackened faces and lifting their children high in their arms to watch the fire burn in the inky night. Laughing and talking in jovial voices until one voice rose above them all: the beautiful clear soprano of Rosa Anderson. For what seemed like minutes she sang out one long, unwavering note which floated up from her lungs and spread over that crowd and beyond them across the empty prairie, the hymn of their longing and their renunciation and their bittersweet goodbye.

As if to punctuate the song, at that moment distant explosions thundered across the prairie, and they could see spouts of sparks rise high into the air beyond the town. It was dynamite, stored in casks in the cellar of the mine warehouse, exploding belatedly like fireworks, and with each new blast a cheer went up.

And let us imagine, finally, that God was looking down upon Sims that night, as those unburdened people stood on the far edge of the river on the far edge of the century, in the middle of those great plains in the middle of this vast continent, unterrified, laughing and singing and slaughtering goats for a midnight feast under the starblown sky. Let us imagine that God watched as Thorsten Larsen tightened the strings of his Hardanger fiddle and they began to dance.

And indeed He might have been watching, because that fire burned strong and luminous on the dark prairie, burned long into the morning, a spectacle bright enough to catch even the oldest and most tired eyes.

Some People Let You Down

Halloween fell on a Saturday the year I was ten, which I remember because Saturdays were the days that my father came to pick me up at the house where, until recently, we had all lived together, and where now my mother and I lived by ourselves. That morning, I sat waiting at the kitchen table while my mother stood by the sink, smoking and looking out the window. His absence from our house was still new enough that I often thought of him in an anticipatory way—a lingering sense that he was always about to walk through the kitchen door, whistling whatever song had last been on the radio—but only on Saturdays did we actually wait. The house was much quieter now.

Neither of my parents had said anything about Halloween, even though it was my favorite holiday. I took my costumes very seriously, driving my mother crazy with my demands. The year before, I'd gone as Sandy from *Grease*—my father had let me rent it at the video store, despite the PG-13 rating—and we'd driven all the way to Garden City to find a black leather jacket in my size. But, since my father had moved out, I'd learned that it was better to keep my expectations low than to suffer daily disappointments, and I hadn't brought it up, either. The world, it seemed, had turned against me. In the kitchen, I stirred my cereal, examining the changing pattern of Cheerios: signs and portents. The kitchen steeped in sallow light.

When we heard his car pull into the driveway, my mother said, "He's here," and dropped her cigarette into the sink. "Are you ready?"

I stood and shouldered my overnight bag.

"Have a good day, sweetheart." She knelt beside me, kissed my cheek. "And Abby?"

My mother smelled pleasantly of sleep and smoke. She was wearing her pink bathrobe, hair loose, eyes heavy. Saturdays were her only days to sleep in, and I knew that as soon as I was gone, she'd go back to bed for an hour or two. "What?" I said.

She sighed and smiled thinly. "Be nice to him, okay?"

■ ■

In the driveway, my father waited in his old wood-paneled Chrysler.

"Ahoy, honey," he said when I opened the door, our old joke. "Climb aboard."

"Hi, Dad."

He was wearing what I thought of as his weekend clothes—jeans, boots, brown hunting jacket—and his face was rough with stubble. As usual, the radio was tuned to 92 Rock.

"Pancakes at Patti's?" he said, and I nodded even though I'd already had cereal. This new Saturday arrangement had been in place for several weeks, and by now I understood the drill: our day would consist of an elaborately choreographed series of activities designed to avoid, as long as possible, returning to the drab apartment—warped linoleum, sagging Goodwill sofa, radiator hiss that kept me up at night—he now occupied above the dry cleaners on Main Street.

My father lingered for a moment before backing out of the driveway, looking out the windshield at the house. "You guys haven't raked," he said. The small lawn was bright with the maple's dropped leaves.

He waited, as though expecting an answer.

"No," I said.

"I'll stay and help when I drop you off tomorrow." He pursed his lips. "I bet the gutters need clearing, too."

■ ■

Patti's was as busy that day as I'd ever seen it. As I followed my father to the small table in the far corner where we always sat, I scanned the room and saw, among the familiar faces from town, several farm families who'd driven in for the day to eat and shop and socialize. They were easy to pick out: parents dressed up as though for church, crowded by their many assorted children, whose nearly indistinguishable faces hovered above the table. Some of the children were already in costume—I saw a lion, a skeleton, and a home-sewn Superman—and I knew they'd have to wear these costumes around all day, waiting until it grew late enough for a quick round of trick-or-treating before their parents drove them back to the farm. Our town was no metropolis, but it was the only concentration of people in the county, and living in town gave me a certain self-importance. I felt immediately, disdainfully sorry for the farm children in their daylight costumes, which was a welcome reprieve from feeling sorry for myself.

After a few minutes, Patti appeared with a cup of coffee for my father and an orange juice for me. She was wearing bright red lipstick and a pair of devil's horns on her head.

"Quite a crowd you've got in here today," my father said.

Patti winked at him. "Keeps me young," she said, and vanished.

He turned his attention to me. "So, how're rehearsals?"

This was a touchy subject. The school play that year was *Annie*, and I'd had my eye on the title role for months. I'd paid my dues, worked my way up from "Lost girl" in our first-grade production of *Peter Pan* to Liesel in *The Sound of Music* last year. That summer, before he moved out, my father and I had run our own private rehearsals in the basement. We'd listened to the tape over and over again, running lines, practicing pitch, and I'd shown up to the auditions in September with the script already memorized, smug and imperious and ready for glory.

But when Mrs. Bazner assigned the roles, standing on the stage of our school's little theater and reading the names off her list, she gave Annie to Melinda Chase, and I waited in stunned disbelief for my name to be called, several orphans down the line. When I heard that I'd been cast as Tessie—she of the childish mood swings and the imbecilic catchphrase, "Oh my goodness"—it felt as though some membrane inside me had torn. Hot tears leaked from my eyes and, furious with shame, I hurried out of the theater. With nowhere else to go, I hid in a stall in the bathroom, where for the first time since my father left, I cried with abandon.

Mrs. Bazner came to find me after a while. "Abby?" she called into the bathroom. I didn't answer, but she didn't leave. I could see her scuffed black clogs beneath the stall door.

"It's a good part, Abby," she said, finally. "Tessie's the comic relief. I couldn't trust anyone else to play her."

This was no real comfort, but I wiped my face with toilet paper and came out of the stall. Mrs. Bazner knelt down and took me in her arms. She was a kind woman. I'd known her since kindergarten, but that was the first time I can remember being alone with her. Up close, she smelled like hairspray.

"I know things are hard right now," she said into my ear, and I stiffened. It wasn't yet apparent to me how public the troubles in my family had become, but Mrs. Bazner clearly knew something about them, and it was the embarrassment of this, even more than being passed over for Annie, that made it impossible for me to return to rehearsals after that. That was the day that I began to notice people looking at me in a new, pitying way, and I understood our troubles were well-known, talked about in line at the Post Office, I imagined, and at bridge games, and at Sunday lunches after church.

That was all more than a month ago, but I hadn't yet told my father that I'd quit the play. In the tumult of those weeks, I'd simply allowed him to assume, without telling him outright, that I'd won the title role, and now it had become a heavy, agonizing secret. Every time it came up, I remembered those afternoons in the basement, singing "I Don't Need Anything but You" as a duet, his thin voice filling the low-ceilinged room, always a little flat. Really, he had no singing voice at all.

"Fine," I said, and before he could ask anything else, Patti arrived with our usual order. "One stack of blueberry, whipped cream on the side," she said.

My father thanked her and pointed to his head, indicating her devil horns. "What's with the . . . ?"

Patti smiled, baring white teeth through her red-painted lips. "Think they suit me?"

His puzzled expression didn't change, and Patti and I realized at the same time that he didn't understand. She released an exasperated sigh.

"Oh, Cam. It's Halloween."

He frowned and looked out at the restaurant again: through his eyes I took in, for the second time, the ghosts and superheroes around us. "Well, I'll be damned," he said.

I flushed with shame. My father's attention was always selective: he remembered that the trash needed to go out on Wednesday but woke up and dressed for work on Saturdays by mistake. He noticed that the leaves hadn't been raked but forgot that it was Halloween. My mother and I made fun of him: he lost his keys; he lost his wallet. He was always finding forgotten bills in his pockets, creased windfalls he'd use to take us all out for ice cream. Before, these little lapses had been part of his charm, but now they felt part of some larger negligence. What would he forget next? My birthday?

My father looked embarrassed, too. Patti knelt down so that her eyes were level with mine. The look she gave me was both playful and serious. "Abby," she said, "your dad doesn't really belong in this world, does he?" She smiled, leaned in conspiratorially, and whispered: "That's why he needs our help."

Her tone was so similar to the one my mother had used in the kitchen earlier that morning—"Be nice to him, okay?"—that I frowned at her in surprise.

"The horns are all wrong," my father told her. "You're an angel."

She rolled her eyes and vanished again.

In the silence that followed, I looked at him across the table. His face was the same kindly face that had smiled at me across our breakfast table at home on so many mornings. Not quite the same, though. The smile a little pinched, perhaps. His cheeks unshaven. My shame melted into anger. *I* needed help. Who was helping *me*?

"Are you growing a beard?" I asked him, sneering.

"Thought I might," he said. And, without missing a beat, he clapped a hand to his eye for a patch and flashed his old pirate smirk. "What say you, lubber? Think it suits me?"

■ ■

After breakfast, we walked out into the cool morning, which smelled of manure blown off the fields outside of town and also, vaguely, of smoke.

Now we would go visit my grandmother, who lived alone in a bungalow on 3rd Street. Once pleasant enough, these weekly visits had become ordeals. My grandmother's disappointment in my father bordered on denial. "I just don't understand why you and Katie can't work things out," she'd say, inevitably, five minutes into our visit. "Everybody *quarrels!* That's half of marriage!"

We'd be sitting in her living room, still blinking to adjust to the dim, thick-curtained light. On the coffee table: a tray of Oreos and at least two ashtrays, since my grandmother almost never took a breath without a Parliament between her lips. On the radio: baseball. Or, since baseball season was over: talk radio.

My father would sigh and try to change the subject. "Mom, did you know that Abby's the lead in the school play this year?"

"Is she? Well, that's wonderful, sweetheart," she'd say. Then, sadly, smokily: "I never thought it would last this long. I told everybody. They'll have it worked out in a week, I said. You'll see."

I could see how this kind of badgering tortured my father, but I thought my grandmother had a point. My parents had not yet offered much explanation for their separation. All I was told, on that terrible day when they sat me down in the living room, was that they no longer wanted to live together, though they loved me very much, and, they admitted under interrogation, loved each other, too. But the small evidence of marital distress I'd witnessed in my short life seemed vastly outweighed by the heartache I'd seen since—my mother crying in the laundry room, my father's sad apartment—not to mention the trouble they'd caused me. At that early stage, it still seemed possible that any day they might come to their senses and correct their mistake.

My father would endure her harangue for half an hour or so, and we'd leave in time to catch the matinee at the

Showplace Theatre. That afternoon, I knew, they were showing *Night of the Living Dead.*

But before we got into the car in Patti's parking lot, I heard someone yell my name. When I turned, Melinda Chase was bounding happily towards us. Behind her, I saw her parents emerging from their Cadillac.

"Hey, Mel! How's the arm?" my father said. He'd coached our Little League softball teams since we were six. "You keeping in shape in the off-season?"

"Yes, coach!" Melinda said brightly. She turned to me. "Are you coming trick-or-treating tonight?"

I searched her face for any trace of guile, of subterfuge. Then, finding none, I felt ashamed for my suspicion. She'd never said anything unkind to me. We'd been friends. We *were* friends. We'd gone trick-or-treating together the year before, and the year before that, and the year before that with our mothers in tow. Since quitting the play, since learning how public my parents' divorce had become, I'd avoided all my other school friends, Melinda especially. I'd felt their eyes on me—watchful, pitying, even mocking—and so I'd adopted a defiant standoffishness. But now, in a hopeful flash, it occurred to me that perhaps the estrangement I'd felt at school in the last few weeks was just the product of my imagination, a kind of self-imposed exile. I imagined a night of trick-or-treating with her and the other girls, shrieking up and down the streets, collecting candy in our pillowcases, then going back to her house and dumping our hauls on her bedroom floor to compare.

But, of course, I didn't have a costume. And anyway, it was supposed to be my day with my father, who was smiling at us over the top of the Chrysler. "I don't know," I told her in a low voice.

"Mel! Come on, now!" From across the parking lot, her father's voice was firm, urgent.

"Gotta go," she said. "See you tonight."

"Don! Kathy!" my father shouted genially, waving to her parents. "Careful! It's a madhouse in there!"

Stiffly, Melinda's father lifted his hand. His bald head gleamed in the bright October sun. Her mother stood scowling in her print dress. He was a deacon in our church. She was the librarian in our town's fusty little library. In the brief moment before her father dropped his hand and they turned and disappeared into Patti's, I watched their faces change, warp, as though by some terrible mask, and I saw there, quite clearly, the same pitying disdain that I'd just naively hoped away.

■■

Hunkered down in my shame, I didn't notice that we'd missed the turn to 3rd Street until we were already near the edge of town.

"Dad? Where are we going?"

He smiled. "We forgot to get our pumpkins!"

I'd forgotten, too. Every year, my parents and I drove out of town to the pumpkin stand that Mr. Erickson ran on his farm, where we each picked a pumpkin to carve.

"What about grandma?" I asked.

"She'll keep."

Peering down the side streets, I saw three or four thin threads of grey smoke rising into the bright sky: leaf-piles,

burning in backyards. Then we turned onto the old highway and the fields opened up before us, vast and vacant,
October-brown. Soon, I knew, the winter wheat would
sprout and turn them an eerie, iridescent green.

The Erickson farm was about fifteen minutes outside of
town. As we drove, I could still feel the looks that Melinda's
parents had aimed at us, and I was as sad and self-pitying
as I think I'd ever been. But the mood inside the car was
strange, discordant: "Gimme Shelter" was playing on the
radio, and my father was singing happily under his breath,
keeping time with his palm on the steering wheel.

Mr. Erickson's farm stand was just a long piece of plywood spanning two sawhorses with a hand-painted sign
that said, "Carving Pumpkins! Indian Corn! Fresh Eggs!"
As we pulled to the roadside and parked next to the field of
dried cornstalks, I saw that it was presently manned by one
of Mr. Erickson's large, square-headed sons.

"Howdy," my father said as we walked over. "Here to
browse your pumpkins."

My father taught social studies at the high school and I
wondered if he might know the boy, but he didn't seem to.

"That's all we got left," the boy said, pointing to a
wooden crate beside the stand. At the bottom of the
crate, I could see six or seven wretched, dirty pumpkins.
Every other year, we'd had a beautiful variety to choose
from. But this year we were late. My father rustled around
in the crate, pulled out two of them, and placed them
on the makeshift counter. I cringed. Signs and portents:
the pumpkins were hideous, small and misshapen. They
looked like shrunken heads.

"These'll do!" my father said. "How much?"

The boy said a number and my father opened his wallet to pay, and just then, a figure in overalls appeared out of the cornfield behind the farm stand. I was startled. It was Mr. Erickson, who'd emerged from a narrow path in the corn that I hadn't noticed before.

"Hey, Lee," my father greeted him. "Happy Halloween." He gestured to the absurd pumpkins, which leered at us. "Better late than never, right?"

Mr. Erickson looked at us blankly for a moment. He wore a faded blue baseball hat that threw a shadow across his sun-stained face, and he was carrying something in his hands, a piece of farm equipment I didn't recognize, some kind of sprayer: insectoid, sinister. His voice, when it emerged from his head, was like the sharp creak of a door. "Take your pumpkins and get the hell out of here," he said.

A cool wind rolled over us. The cornstalks shivered, dry and brittle. On all sides of us, the empty fields flung themselves out to the sky. Nothing to cling to, big enough to drown in.

Slowly, the boy looked from his father to mine. I followed his gaze. My father's expression was unreadable. After a moment, he looked down at his wallet, pulled out a bill, and handed it to the boy, who took it without speaking, his mouth gaping.

"Let's go, Abby," my father said. "Take your pumpkin."

As we walked away, Mr. Erickson's voice hit our backs like a spray of gravel: "We don't want to see you out here again, Cam. Here's a family place. You stay in town with the rest of your kind."

We got into the car. Without speaking, my father
started the engine, put it in gear, and pulled back onto the
highway. As we passed the farm stand, I looked out at Mr.
Erickson and his dough-faced son, whose lip had raised in
a snicker.

I remember that look. That boy had a bad mouth. He
had fat, squirming lips that wanted to crawl off his face.

▪▪

We drove in silence. My father hadn't taken the time to
turn the car around, and we were driving east, away from
town. I'm sure the radio was on, but I didn't hear it. The
air in the car was thick and liquid; it clogged my ears.
My father was driving fast. His face was closed, his jaw
set. He stared straight ahead through the windshield and
didn't speak. Outside, the fields flew by endlessly, and it
seemed to me as though we could drive out into them forever without arriving anywhere. Eventually, I thought, we
would simply disappear.

I don't know how long we drove like that—ten minutes, thirty—but after a while the pressure in the car began
to leak out. Slowly, the sound came back—Phil Collins:
mournful, yearning—and the car slowed down to a normal
speed. But then it kept slowing down. I looked at my father
again, and that face haunts me, too. Some cord in his head
had gone slack: his mouth was open, his head sagged, his
eyes were loose and listing. He seemed to have taken his
foot off the gas.

I snapped my eyes forward and saw a sign that said,
"Welcome to the Town of Woods, Kansas (Unincorporated),"

and as the car slowed to a stop in a dusty pull-off next to the highway, I saw that it was not really a town: just a few abandoned buildings, three or four old houses and a barn, all left to sag and buckle in the wind. I had probably driven past it a dozen times, but I'd never noticed it before.

My father put the car in park and we sat there in silence for a few moments, the engine humming, the dust breathing up gently around us.

"Dad?" I ventured, then stopped, unsure what question I wanted to ask, exactly.

He turned away, let out a sob, and covered his face with his hands.

Until that moment, I'd been so consumed by the toll my parents' divorce was taking on me that I'd never really considered the toll it was taking on my father. Now, suddenly, that toll was clear, and terrifying. I was frozen, heart hammering in my chest. I wanted to say something, but I didn't know what to say. I wanted badly for that moment to end. But his crying only intensified, coming now in ragged gasps, which he tried unsuccessfully to stifle. His feelings seemed to have a life of their own. That sound, the sound of him fighting against his sadness and losing: it was the sound of despair itself.

I couldn't stand it; I looked away, out the window at those ruined buildings. Our part of Kansas was full of towns like this, places where a few farm families came together at the intersection of their land before it was all bought up by some big company and they drifted away. The roof of one of the houses was caved in. The paint on the buildings had been stripped by the weather and they'd all faded back to the same sad shade of brown. The place had obviously been vacant for years, but it still had an atmosphere of hasty abandonment, flight. For a wild, panicked moment, I considered opening the door and getting out of the car, leaving him there and running off to take cover in one of the forsaken houses, where I'd live out the rest of my days in hiding from that feeling.

"Oh, kiddo," my father said finally, breaking the spell. I looked at him, relieved. He blew his nose in his handkerchief and took a deep breath. His eyes were still shining, but a sad smile played around his lips, a sign that the moment was truly over. "Some people let you down, you know?"

I thought he was apologizing. For his outburst, for scaring me, but also, maybe, for more than that. For leaving us, for ruining the way things were. Anyway, that's what I wanted to hear. I was anxious to receive an apology, and, surprising myself a little, anxious to accept one.

"It's okay," I said, and then, surprising myself again: "Dad, I quit the play."

He blinked, furrowed his brow. "How come?"

"I got Tessie. Melinda got Annie."

"Oh, honey," he said, his voice thick with sympathy. "I'm so sorry."

"It's okay," I said again.

And that was it. As if to mark the boundary of our misery, Diana Ross came on the radio. My father and I shared a small smile. Then he put the car in gear, turned around, and headed back to town.

On the way, we had to drive past the Erickson farm stand. My father either didn't notice or pretended not to—he stared straight ahead at the road, humming along to the radio—but I couldn't help looking out at the Erickson boy. I think I understood, even then, that something truly horrible had happened, but I could only grasp the edges of it. As we drove past, I scrutinized his face, searching for a clue. The sneer was gone, replaced by nothing, blankness. He stared off into space without seeming to register our car. Sitting there by the highway, surrounded by those empty fields, I remember thinking that he looked lonely, or lost.

■■

I've been thinking about that day, turning it over in my mind, since a conversation I had last week with my mother. We've been talking on the phone more often since my husband moved out. For now, I'm staying in the house by myself, and some evenings it fills up with a silence I can't stand. Usually, we talk about our days, the news, the novel she checked out of the library, but that night, for the first time, it occurred to me to ask what it was like for her when my father moved out.

"Well, that was a hard time for all of us," she said. "It was terrible for you, of course. And while I can't say that I was surprised when he came out, I was still hurt, and angry." She paused for a moment, then went on: "I remember one night, one of those nights when you were at your father's, I got drunk and decided to throw all of his things away, whatever was left in the house. So I went around with a garbage bag in one hand and a glass of wine in the other. There was some low-hanging fruit: some clothes in the basement, his old pipe set, his roller skates. But after that, it wasn't so easy. I remember sitting on the living room floor, going through the records, and thinking, 'Well, okay, all these Neil Young albums are Cam's, but I *love* Neil Young, and it isn't fair that I have to throw them out.'" She chuckled. "Then I just gave up. I didn't even throw out the roller skates."

She paused again, pensive. In the lull that followed, I looked around my living room, where the debris of my married years has accumulated. I'm only at the beginning of my own disentanglement, and the balance of it stretched out before me, the end not yet in sight.

Finally, my mother sighed. "Still, I think it was worst for your father," she said. "On top of everything, he'd had his heart broken, too. All that sad business with Mr. Owen . . ."

She thought I already knew. There had been a love affair, she explained at my insistence. Mr. Owen was a traveling seed salesman who was a familiar presence in our town. I had to squint to conjure a picture of him in my mind: handsome, funny, dark hair slicked to the side, white flash of smile, always wearing a tie and good shoes. It had been torrid and anguished and short-lived, but apparently my father had thought it might become something more. He'd confessed to my mother, made a series of overtures to Mr. Owen, was rebuffed and humiliated, and then moved into the apartment above the dry cleaners.

"I'm surprised he never told you," she said again. I'm surprised, too. I suppose he's embarrassed, a thought that pains me. "Well, everything worked out for the best," she said blithely, sheepish about revealing his secret, wanting to put an end to it.

■■

By the time we got back to town that day, we felt better, relieved to have left our sadness behind us. When we opened the door to his apartment above the dry cleaners, we paused for a moment, holding our sad, shriveled pumpkins, looking at the sagging sofa where I'd spend the night, and as if to prevent that sadness from catching up with us, my father crossed the room and turned on the little radio he kept on the bookcase: Fleetwood Mac, our favorite.

He spread newspaper over the dining room table and we sang and talked for an hour while we carved our jack-o'-lanterns. It was cheerful, familiar. When we were finished, we lined them up on the table and stood back to look. They were hideous. They smiled their dark, crooked smiles at us, and they were so ugly that we started laughing, and we laughed until the phone rang.

He picked it up. "Hi, Mom," he said, and then he listened for a long time while my grandmother said whatever she said in her muffled, chiding voice. He rolled his eyes at me. When he finally hung up, the light outside had begun to thicken. I looked again at the jack-o'-lanterns and had an idea.

"Let's go and see her," I said.

"Now?"

I nodded. "They'll start trick-or-treating soon."

When he realized what I was saying, he said, "Well, shiver me timbers," and then we spent half an hour scrounging around for costumes. He found a handkerchief in his sock drawer and tied it around his head like a bandana, then fashioned an eye patch from a rubber band and an old black T-shirt. I didn't have any clothes at his place, so we snuck into the dry cleaners downstairs through the back door, where the clothes of our neighbors hung ghostly in their translucent bags. It didn't take long for me to find something suitable: a frilly white dress that probably belonged to some middle school girl but was only a little too big for me.

We brought it back upstairs and I changed in the bathroom. When I came out, my father looked at me quizzically. "Cinderella?"

"Dad!" I shouted, indignant. "Madonna!"

He pursed his lips, held up a finger, and disappeared into his bedroom. When he came out a moment later, he was holding a marker, which he used to dot a mole over my mouth. We looked in the mirror together, and I did my best to conjure her "Like a Virgin" pout. We laughed. I looked nothing like her—my hair was limp, my lips thin and pale, and I had none of her swagger—but it didn't matter.

We were ready. We got back in the car with our jack-o'-lanterns and drove to my grandmother's house. When she answered the door, frowning at us in our costumes, my father and I yelled, in unison, "Trick or treat!"

Even she got into the spirit. She rooted around in the closet and found an old witch's hat—"It suits you," my father said—and then she filled our pumpkins with tea candles and dug out a bag of old lollipops from her pantry.

We turned on the T.V. and when, every few minutes, the doorbell rang, we all rose and opened the door

together—my father snarling, my grandmother cackling—
and plied our costumed callers with candy. If they were
farm kids, their parents followed along behind them in the
car with their headlights dimmed. And then they vanished
into the night, while we retreated to the smoky living room
to watch *The Creature from the Black Lagoon*.

As the night went on, the trick-or-treaters grew older
and scarcer. My grandmother fell asleep with her cigarette burning down in the ashtray beside her. The living
room was dark. My father and I watched in silence as the
Creature stalked the heedless scientists. I'd never seen
the film before, and I was rapt. But then, during a slow
sequence, I happened to glance over at my father, who sat
across the room, and I saw that he wasn't watching the
movie at all. He was staring down at the carpet, and in the
TV's silver glow, I could see that his face—stubbled jaw,
eyepatch flipped up—was bright with tears.

I held my breath for a moment, watching him. I felt an
urge to go to him, comfort him somehow. But I also sensed
that this was a private moment. In the eerie, lunar light
pouring from the screen, he looked strange, otherworldly.
He was there in the room with me, this man I knew, but
apart, too, unfamiliar and alien. The TV's light flashed and
dimmed, flashed again.

I turned my eyes back to the movie. I don't know how
long we sat like that. It felt like forever, like my whole
childhood. But it couldn't have been that long, because I
remember that, before the movie was over, the doorbell
rang again. Merciful sound, the chime that frees you from
your nightmare.

My grandmother startled awake, coughing. My father rose quickly and turned away, straightening his costume. When he turned back a moment later, his face bore no trace of his tears. Together, we went to the door and answered it, and standing in the porchlight was Melinda, with Amy Caldwell and the Logan twins. They were a coordinated *Star Wars* posse, Luke, Leia, Han and Chewie. Melinda was Leia, her hair pinned up in perfect buns.

"Abby, hi!" she said in friendly surprise, and then her brow knit with a question.

"Madonna," I explained preemptively.

"Oh!" she said. "Cool!" We'd watched the music video a hundred times in her basement. "Do you want to come with us?" she asked, lifting her heavy pillowcase. "We're almost done."

"No, thanks," I said. "See you Monday."

As they walked away, my father shouted after them, "I'm counting down the days until next season, girls. I want that trophy!"

"Yes, Coach," they called back over their shoulders.

We stood in the doorway for a moment, watching them walk away. "She'll be good," he said. "But you would've been better."

■ ■

My mother's right, of course: everything worked out for the best. My father recently retired from teaching at a school in Denver, where he's lived for many years with a kind, soft-spoken accountant named Otto. My mother's remarried, too, to George Henderson, who was our mayor for a while when I was a kid. Last year, we all had Christmas together, my parents and George and Otto and me, crowded into my father's living room, where we opened gifts and sang carols in cracked harmony. None of us can sing at all except for George, whose tenor broke through our racket, so clear and sweet that we all shut up to listen.

But before all that, there were bad years. The spring following that Halloween, my father was asked to step down as coach of our softball team, and then, after some parents threatened to take their children out of his classroom, he lost his job at the school on an elaborately constructed pretext. He stuck it out for a couple of months, working night shifts at the gas station, but he couldn't keep that up forever, and he moved to Denver in the fall.

By then, my parents had told me that my father was gay. It felt like I was the last to know. They wanted to protect me, I'm sure, and assumed that they could keep it secret. But secrets didn't last long in our town. This revelation illuminated some recent mysteries, while at the same time making the future seem opaque and uncertain. I'd heard about gay men, but I didn't know any. Though I was beginning to see glimpses of it, I was still largely shielded from the world of adults: the world in which, I would soon learn, people were quite concerned about contagion, AIDS, child abuse, and hell. My primary association with the word was that older boys at schools sometimes used it to insult each other.

"It's nothing wrong, Abby," my mother said. "It's nothing to be ashamed of."

"It doesn't change anything between us," my father said, looking me in the eye. "Things between us will stay just the same as they are."

I'm sure he meant that. I'm sure he intended to stay in our town, keep his job and his sad apartment, and continue our Saturday routine indefinitely. He believed in people.

When he came to say goodbye to me a few months later, car packed with his few possessions, I reminded him of that promise. "You said things would stay the same," I sobbed. "You promised."

He knelt down and hugged me. I remember his stubble against my cheek, the wetness of his tears.

"I know, honey," he said. "I'm so sorry. I'm so sorry. I'm so sorry."

I've never forgiven myself for that.

"Some people let you down," my father told me, swamped with heartache by that abandoned town, the day I saw my first glimpse of true horror. And I have certainly found that to be true.

But not of him.

Acknowledgments

These stories first appeared, some in slightly different form, in the following publications: "Woods, Kansas" in *Crazyhorse;* "Pestilence" in *Indiana Review;* "Two Floods" in *The Florida Review;* "Summer People" in *Colorado Review;* "Destiny" in *Gulf Coast;* "Prairie Fire, 1899" in *One Story.* Deep gratitude to the editors of those journals.

Profound thanks to Karen DeVinney, Bess Whitby, and Andy Briseño at the University of North Texas Press for all their work to make the dream of this book into a reality.

While writing this book, I received generous support from the Bread Loaf Writers Conference, the James Merrill House, the Jentel Foundation, the Jerome Foundation, the MacDowell Colony, the Minnesota State Arts Board, the Ucross Foundation, the Vermont Studio Center, and the Virginia Center for the Creative Arts.

I owe an incalculable debt to my teachers and mentors. To Emily Bayer, Kiese Laymon, David Means, Julie Schumacher, and Alexander Chee: thank you for sharing your wisdom and kindness with me. To Charles Baxter and Paul Russell: this book would not have been possible without you.

These stories benefited immensely from the insight of dozens of readers. Thank you to my colleagues and friends at the University of Minnesota, especially Jonathan Atkinson, John Costello, and Su Hwang, whose brilliance helped shape this book. Thank you also to members of the After School Collective, especially Connor Stratton, Anna Rasmussen, and Alexandra Watson, who read draft after draft of these stories. I couldn't be more grateful for your art and your friendship.

To Jennifer Bowen, and to all the teachers, mentors, and students with Minnesota Prison Writing Workshop: thank you for reminding me every day how art can help shape the future we want, a future without walls or bars.

To Kristin Collier, always, for everything.